Dear Reader,

Readers sometimes ask me where I got my start as a writer. When I tell people that my first novels were romantic comedies for Bantam's Loveswept line, they're usually quite surprised. Although this genre may seem completely different from the suspense I write now, the two have more in common than it seems.

For me, every good story has two essential elements to it: characters to fall in love with and root for, and a mystery to figure out—whether it is an unsolved crime or that baffling and bewildering emotion that puzzles us most of all—love. Even the most intricate murder plot can't compare to the complex inner workings of the human heart.

In *Reilly's Return*, Pat Reilly is a sexy Australian movie star who is used to ladies throwing themselves at his feet. But the one woman who holds Pat's heart was married to his best friend, and now is mourning her husband's death. Pat promised that he would give Jayne Jordan time to grieve, but a man can only stay away from his love for so long. Just as Jayne thinks she's finally settled into her life after her husband's passing, writing movie reviews in an idyllic coastal town, Pat comes storming back into her life. Can Jayne give herself over to this dangerously handsome man without loosing her head and her heart?

Pat and Jayne's story brings us back to the small town featured in my Rainbow Chasers trilogy that captured my imagination years ago. I hope that you'll enjoy this story as much today as I did at the very beginning of my writing career.

All my best,

Tami Hoag

Tami Hoag

PRAISE FOR THE BESTSELLERS OF

Tami Hoag

THE ALIBI MAN

"Captivating thriller . . . [Elena] is a heroine readers will want to see more of."

—*Publishers Weekly*

"Hard to put down."

—*The Washington Post*

"A superbly taut thriller. Written in a staccato style that will have readers racing through the pages . . . will leave readers breathless and satisfied."

—*Booklist*

"A suspenseful tale, with a surprising ending, the author once again has constructed a hard-hitting story with interesting characters and a thrilling plot."

—*The Midwest Book Review*

"Elena Estes [is] one of Hoag's most complicated, difficult and intriguing characters . . . Hoag enhances a tight mystery plot with an over-the-shoulder view of the Palm Beach polo scene, giving her readers an up-close-and-personal look at the rich and famous . . . *The Alibi Man* is her best work to date."

—www.BookReporter.com

PRIOR BAD ACTS

"A snappy, scary thriller."

—*Entertainment Weekly*

"Stunning . . . Here [Hoag] stands above the competition, creating complex characters who evolve more than those in most thrillers. The breathtaking plot twists are perfectly paced in this compulsive page-turner."

—*Publishers Weekly* (starred review)

"A chilling thriller with a romantic chaser."

—*Daily News*

"A first-rate thriller with an ending that will knock your socks off."

—*Booklist*

"An engrossing thriller with plenty of plot twists and a surprise ending."

—*OK! Magazine*

"A chilling tale of murder and mayhem."

—*BookPage*

"The in-depth characterization and the unrelenting suspense are what makes [this] an outstanding read. Gritty and brutal at times, *Prior Bad Acts* delivers a stunning novel of murder, vengeance and retribution . . . riveting and chilling suspense."

—*Romance Reviews Today*

KILL THE MESSENGER

"Excellent pacing and an energetic plot heighten the suspense . . . enjoyable."

—*Chicago Tribune*

"Everything rings true, from the zippy cop-shop banter, to the rebellious bike messenger subculture, to the ultimate, heady collision of Hollywood money, politics, and power."

—*Minneapolis Star Tribune*

"Hoag's usual crisp, uncluttered storytelling and her ability to make us care about her characters triumphs in *Kill the Messenger*."

—*Fort Lauderdale Sun-Sentinel*

"A perfect book. It is well written, and it has everything a reader could hope for. . . . It cannot be put down. . . . Please don't miss this one."

—*Kingston Observer* (MA)

"[A] brisk read . . . it demonstrates once again why [Hoag's] so good at what she does."

—*San Francisco Chronicle*

"Action-filled ride . . . a colorful, fast-paced novel that will keep you guessing."

—*The Commercial Appeal*

"High octane suspense . . . Non-stop action moves the story forward at a breath-stealing pace, and the tension remains high from beginning to end . . . suspense at its very best."

—*Romance Reviews Today*

"Hoag's loyal readers and fans of police procedural suspense novels will definitely love it."

—*Booklist*

"Engaging . . . the triumph of substance over style . . . character-driven, solidly constructed thriller."

—*Publishers Weekly*

"Hoag upholds her reputation as one of the hottest writers in the suspense genre with this book, which not only has a highly complex mystery, multi-layered suspense and serpentine plot, but also great characterizations . . . an entertaining and expertly crafted novel not to be missed."

—*Curled Up with a Good Book*

DARK HORSE

"A thriller as tightly wound as its heroine . . . Hoag has created a winning central figure in Elena . . . Bottom line: Great ride."

—*People*

"This is her best to date . . . [a] tautly told thriller."

—*Minneapolis Star-Tribune*

"Hoag proves once again why she is considered a queen of the crime thriller."

—*Charleston Post & Courier*

"A tangled web of deceit and double-dealing makes for a fascinating look into the wealthy world of horses juxtaposed with the realistic introspection of one very troubled ex-cop. A definite winner."

—*Booklist*

"Anyone who reads suspense novels regularly is acquainted with Hoag's work—or certainly should be. She's one of the most consistently superior suspense and romantic suspense writers on today's bestseller lists. A word of warning to readers: don't think you know whodunit 'til the very end."

—*The Facts* (Clute, TX)

"Suspense, shocking violence, and a rip-roaring con-
clusion—this novel has all the pulse-racing touches
that put Tami Hoag books on bestseller lists and crime
fans' reading lists."

—*The Advocate Magazine* (Baton Rouge, LA)

"Full of intrigue, glitter, and skullduggery. . . . [Hoag]
is a master of suspense."

—*Publishers Weekly*

"Her best to date, an enjoyable read, and a portent of
even better things to come."

—*The Grand Rapids Press*

"A complex cerebral puzzle that will keep readers on
the edge until all the answers are revealed."

—*The Midwest Book Review*

"To say that Tami Hoag is the absolute best at what
she does is a bit easy since she is really the only person
who does what she does. . . . It is testament to Hoag's
skill that she is able to go beyond being skillful and
find the battered hearts in her characters, and capture
their beating on the page. . . . A superb read."

—*Detroit News & Free Press*

TAMI HOAG

~

Reilly's Return

BANTAM BOOKS
NEW YORK

2010 Bantam Books Mass Market Edition

Copyright © 1990 by Tami Hoag

Published in the United States by Bantam Books,
an imprint of The Random House Publishing Group,
a division of Random House, Inc., New York.

BANTAM BOOKS and the rooster colophon are registered
trademarks of Random House, Inc.

Originally published in paperback in the United States as
The Rainbow Chasers: Reilly's Return by Bantam Books,
a division of Random House, Inc., in 1990.

978-0-553-80643-4

Printed in the United States of America

www.bantamdell.com

2   4   6   8   9   7   5   3

PROLOGUE

University of Notre Dame, South Bend, Indiana
Spring 1977

"OKAY, EVERYBODY, THIS is it. The final portrait of the Fearsome Foursome. Make sure your caps are on straight, ladies. I'm setting the timer now." Bryan Hennessy hunched over the 3.5-millimeter camera, fussing with buttons and switches, pausing once to push his glasses up on his straight nose.

Jayne Jordan watched him, her dark eyes bright with curiosity and unshed tears. She memorized everything about the moment, Bryan's athletic way of moving, the gentleness of his big hands on the delicate equipment, the way his tawny hair stuck out between his cap and the collar of his shirt. At some later date she would be able to replay this moment through her mind as if it were a movie clip.

Absently she lifted a slim hand in a token attempt at straightening her wild mane of dark auburn hair. Her heart ached at the thought that memories would soon be all she would have of her friends.

Decked out in graduation caps and gowns, they stood on the damp grass near the blue expanse of St. Mary's Lake. The clean, cool air was sweet with the scents of spring flowers, new leaves, and freshly cut grass. Birdsong mingled with Alice Cooper's "School's Out" blasting from a boom box in a distant dorm.

Beside her stood sweet-natured Faith Kincaid—golden hair, golden heart, and an inner peacefulness Jayne had always admired and envied. Beside Faith stood Alaina Montgomery, the group's cynic. Alaina was as practical as the short style of her chestnut hair. She stubbornly refused to believe in anything that couldn't be admitted as evidence in a court of law. Bryan hustled around to stand behind them, his cap askew. He was handsome, sweet, and eccentric. A student of all things mystical and magical, he was her soul mate in many ways. To the group as a whole, Bryan was their surrogate big brother, their confidant.

These were Jayne's three best friends in the world. They were the first people who had ever really understood her, including her own beloved family back in Paris, Kentucky.

They had banded together their freshman year. Four people with nothing in common but a class in medieval sociology. Over the four years that followed they had seen each other through finals and failures, triumphs and tragedies, and doomed romances. They were friends in the truest, deepest sense of the word.

And today they would graduate and go their separate ways.

As hard as she tried, Jayne couldn't be philosophical about it. As eager as she was to plunge into the future, she couldn't help but feel she was being cut adrift.

"Okay. Everybody smile," Bryan ordered, his voice a little huskier than usual. "It's going to go off any second now. Any second."

They all grinned engagingly and held their collective breath.

The camera suddenly tilted downward on its tripod, pointing its lens at one of the white geese that wandered freely around St. Mary's Lake. The shutter clicked and the motor advanced the film. The goose honked an outraged protest and waddled away.

"I hope that's not an omen," Jayne said, frowning as she nibbled at her thumbnail. She was devoutly superstitious, and this certainly didn't look like good luck.

"It's a loose screw," Bryan announced, digging a dime out of his pants pocket to repair the tripod with.

"In Jayne or the camera?" Alaina queried, her cool blue eyes sparkling with teasing mischief.

Jayne made a face at her. "Very funny, Alaina."

"I think it's a sign that Bryan needs a new tripod," said Faith.

"That's not what Jessica Porter says," Alaina remarked slyly.

The girls giggled as Bryan blushed up to the roots of his hair. Outside of this unusual set of friendships with Jayne, Faith, and Alaina, Bryan had led an active social life.

"If you want a sign, look behind you," he said as he fussed unnecessarily with the aperture setting on the camera.

Jayne turned and immediately caught sight of a rainbow arching gracefully across the morning sky above the golden dome of the administration building.

"Oh, how beautiful," Faith said with a sigh.

"Symbolic," Jayne whispered. A tingling feeling raced through her as she admired the soft colors and contemplated the meaning of this moment. A rainbow seemed like a good sign, something to follow and believe in.

"It's the diffusion of light through raindrops," Alaina said flatly.

Bryan looked up from fiddling with the camera to frown at her, his strong jaw jutting forward aggressively. "Rainbows have lots of magic in them," he said, dead serious. "Ask any leprechaun. It'd do you some good to believe in magic, Alaina."

Alaina's lush mouth turned down at the corners. "Take the picture, Hennessy."

Bryan ignored her, his wise, warm blue eyes taking on a dreamy quality as he gazed up at the soft stripes of color. "We'll each be chasing our own rainbows after today. I wonder where they'll lead us."

They each recited the stock answers they'd been giving faculty, friends, and family for months. Bryan had been accepted into the graduate program of parapsychology at Purdue. Faith was heading for a managerial position in a business office in Cincinnati. Alaina was staying on at Notre Dame to attend law school. Jayne was all packed and ready to leave for Hollywood to pursue a career as a writer and director.

"That's where our brains are taking us," Bryan said, pulling his cap off to comb a hand back through his hair as he always did when he went into one of his "deep thinking modes." "I wonder where our hearts would take us."

If anyone knew the answer to that, it was Bryan, Jayne thought. He was the one they told all their secrets to. He was the one who understood her need to find a place of her own, a place where she fit in, a place where she wouldn't be an outsider looking in.

"That's the question we should all be asking ourselves," she said, wagging a slender finger at her friends. "Are we in pursuit of our true bliss, or are we merely following a course charted by the expectations of others?"

"Do we have to get philosophical?" Alaina groaned, rubbing her temples. "I haven't had my mandatory ten cups of coffee yet this morning."

"Life is philosophy, honey," Jayne explained patiently, her voice a slow Kentucky drawl that hadn't altered one iota during the four years she'd spent in northern Indiana. The expression on her delicately sculpted features was almost comically earnest as she tried once again to breach Alaina's wall of practicality. "That's a cosmic reality."

Alaina stared at her, speechless for a full twenty seconds. Finally she said, "We don't have to worry about you. You'll fit right in in California."

Jayne's wide mouth split into a smile, her beautifully carved lips lifting at the corners. Alaina was her opposite in almost every way, which was probably why they understood each other so well. Lord, she was going to miss her friend's sardonic teasing.

"Why, thank you," she said, knowing Alaina would have preferred a spirited argument. She almost giggled at the disgruntled expression her comment received.

Faith chuckled. "Give up, Alaina. You can't win."

Alaina winced and held her hands up as if to ward off the words. "Don't say that. I *abhor* losing."

"Anastasia," Bryan declared loudly. He gave a decisive nod that set the tassel on his cap dancing. The word would have seemed straight out of left field to anyone who didn't know Bryan Hennessy and the workings of his unconventional mind.

Anastasia was the small town on California's rugged northern coast where the four of them had spent spring break. Jayne's eyes misted over at the memory of how they'd fantasized about moving there and pursuing idealistic existences: Bryan had wanted to play the role of local mad scientist; an inn with a view of the ocean had been Faith's wish; they had somehow gotten Alaina to admit to a secret desire to paint; and Jayne had told them all of her dream to have a little farm of her own. It was a desire she'd had ever since she was a child growing up as a tenant in a cottage for hired help on one of Kentucky's prominent thoroughbred farms.

"That's right," Faith said. "We'd all move to Anastasia."

"And live happily ever after." Alaina's tone lacked the sarcasm she had no doubt intended. She sounded wistful instead.

"Even if we never end up there, it's a nice dream," Jayne said softly.

A nice dream. Something to hang on to, like their memories of Notre Dame and each other. Warm, golden images they could hold in a secret place in their hearts to be taken out from time to time when they were feeling lonely or blue.

Jayne reached up to dab a hankie at the tears

that clung to her eyelashes. The memories weren't enough to ease her heart now, and she hadn't even left her friends behind yet. How was she ever going to make it without them? They were her anchors, her rocks, her shoulders to cry on. How could she ever find true happiness without them?

Bryan set the timer on the camera once again then jogged around to stand behind Faith. "Who knows?" he said. "Life is full of crossroads. You can never tell where a path might lead to."

And the camera buzzed and clicked, capturing the Fearsome Foursome—wishful smiles canting their mouths, dreams of the future and tears of parting shining in their eyes as a rainbow arched in the sky behind them—on film for all time.

ONE

REILLY WAS GOING to show up sooner or later. It was fate, destiny, an ominous portent that had appeared in her morning horoscope. She could feel it in the bottom of her belly, that deep, hollow sense of impending doom. She could feel it in the weight of the antique gold bracelet that circled her left wrist with tingling warmth. That was a sure sign.

It wasn't going to matter a bit that she had left Hollywood and moved up the coast to Anastasia—hundreds of miles away from Tinsel Town in more ways than just distance. The year of waiting was over, and he was going to find her.

Jayne Jordan abandoned the wall she'd been washing, dropping her sponge in the metal bucket full of soapy water that sat beside her. Tucking her feet beneath her, she took a deep breath and squeezed her eyes shut as if preparing to dunk her head under water. Heedless of the fact that she was sitting on a scaffolding eight feet above the floor of the stage, she released the air from her lungs and willed herself to relax. Strains of a Mozart serenade floated through her mind as she attempted to banish the sense of dread from her body. Unfortunately, the sweet joyous notes that had poured unblemished from the composer's soul did nothing to erase the image of Pat Reilly from her mind.

She could see him clearly. His image was indelibly etched on her memory. Those breathtaking sky-blue eyes, pale and opalescent, staring out at her from beneath straight dark gold brows; eyes set in a face that was ruggedly masculine. She could feel the intensity of those eyes penetrating her aura, burning through her veneer of restraint and searing her basic feminine core.

It had been that way from their first meeting, and she had cursed both him and herself for it. It had been that way at their last meeting, and it would be that way again, once he found her. And he *would* find her. Pat Reilly was many things, not all of them admirable, but he was nothing if not a man of his word.

Jayne could still feel the mist on her face. She could see the green of the hills and the gray of her husband's headstone and Reilly as he'd stood before her with the collar of his leather jacket turned up against the wind. She could still taste his kiss, the only kiss they had ever shared, a kiss full of compassion and passion, wanting and guilt, sweetness and hunger. And she could hear his voice—that low, velvety baritone with the Australian lilt that never faded, vowing that in a year's time he would return to her. When they both had had a chance to lay Joseph MacGregor's ghost to rest, he would be back.

The year was up.

Jayne sucked in another deep breath as a wave of panic crashed over her. In a valiant effort to fight off the feelings and the memories, she pinched her thumbs and forefingers together to make two circles, held her hands out before her, and began chanting. "Oooommm . . . oooommm . . . oooommm . . ."

The community theater was empty for the moment. Because she hadn't been able to sleep, Jayne had shown up at the crack of dawn to begin cleaning up the building that had stood unused for the past six years. But it wouldn't have mattered if there had been a hundred people present. She would have gone right on chanting had her entire staff of volunteers been gathered around. When a person needed to meditate, a person needed to meditate. It wasn't good for a body to block out its spiritual needs.

"Oooommm . . . oooommm . . . oooommm . . ."

She scrunched her eyebrows together in an expression of absolute concentration and oooommmed for all she was worth, but it didn't do a darn bit of good. In the theater of her mind the memories played out, undaunted, in all their Technicolor glory. Memories of Reilly proved to be as stubborn as the man himself.

The theater was dark and dank, an unpleasant contrast to the sunny spring morning outside. Pat Reilly ignored the atmosphere. His mind was on more important things than the musty state of the auditorium. He ignored the clutter of junk that had been piled haphazardly backstage, stepping over and around the stuff when necessary, but barely sparing it a glance.

He had followed Jayne Jordan's trail to Anastasia, wondering how long it would take actually to track her down once he got there. But luck had been with him. Driving into the picture postcard coastal village, he had spotted her car—a vintage red convertible MG—slanted drunkenly into a parking spot on a side street with one chrome-spoked wheel on the curb.

If he'd had any doubts about the vehicle being

hers—and he hadn't because only Jayne would desecrate the beauty of an antique car with a Save Catalina's Wild Goats bumper sticker—the building the car was parked beside would have settled the question. The marquee was missing several letters, making the building look like an old crone whose teeth were dropping out one by one, but there was enough of the words left so they were understandable. It was the Anastasia Community Theater—a fitting place to find the woman he was looking for.

Now he wound his way through the rubble to the stage proper, following a weird chanting sound. That would be Jayne, he thought, a wry grin tugging at his mouth. The glue beneath the false beard he wore pulled at his skin and he winced. Damn, he probably should have taken five minutes to peel off the disguise. It was his fans he was trying to hide from, not Jayne.

He'd done enough hiding from Jayne and his attraction to her. The time had come for both of them to face facts. Mac was dead and there was nothing standing in their way. It was time to face this damnable attraction that had burned between them from the first time they'd laid eyes on each other, this attraction both of them had denied and cursed and fought against. She had been his best friend's bride, and Lord knew Pat Reilly would sooner have died than betray a mate. But Mac was gone now. A year had passed since they'd laid him to rest. And there was no reason for the living to go on feeling guilty.

He stopped in the wings, stage left, his booted feet spread slightly. He jammed his big hands at the waist of his well-worn jeans and shook his head as he got his first look at the woman he had come there to find.

Jayne sat atop a rickety-looking scaffolding, her legs twisted into a impossible pretzel design that probably had something to do with yoga or some equally mystical malarkey. She was just as he remembered her: pretty in a way that had nothing to do with cosmetics or fashion. Especially not fashion. Jayne's outfits would have made any other woman look like a refugee from Goodwill. This morning she wore gray thermal underwear bottoms, a purple T-shirt, and a man's gray plaid sport coat that swallowed up her petite frame.

Still, she looked damned appealing to Reilly, proving that hers was an inner beauty that was enhanced by delicate features and eyes like huge pools of obsidian. Her hair was spread around her shoulders in a dark auburn cloud that was nearly black in this light and so wild, Reilly would have bet she couldn't get a comb through it to save her life. But it was soft and silky. He knew because he'd once buried his hands in it. He'd dreamed of it nearly every night since; every night for a year.

"Oooommm . . . oooommm . . ." she chanted, her face a study in concentration as Reilly moved closer.

She had a beautifully sculpted mouth. It was wide and expressive with full, ripe lips. Painted a lush shade of mulberry, those lips curved seductively around the *O* sound she made and closed softly on the *M*. Reilly's skin warmed and his mouth went dry as he stared. He could remember exactly the texture and taste of those lips, though he'd sampled them only once, and he had certainly kissed a dozen women since. It was Jayne's taste that lingered on his tongue, sweet and sad and frightened, full of longing and guilt and loneliness. He had craved that taste as if it had been wine. Its memory had haunted him just as the memory of her sweet Kentucky drawl had haunted him.

Memories of Jayne had haunted him more than memories of Mac had, but the thing that had haunted him most was guilt. Now that he saw her, he was all through feeling guilty.

Dang it all, Jayne grumbled inwardly, this wasn't working at all. She was supposed to be relaxing and finding inner peace, centering her being with the cosmos, forgetting about Reilly. Ha! If anything, her premonition about him was growing even stronger. Her bracelet was like an anchor fastened around her wrist, heavy with warning. Why, it was as if he were in the same room with her! It was as if those incredible fluorescent blue eyes of his were boring into her, burning away her sense of self.

If he ever did show up, she was going to be in big trouble. She'd known from the first he was more man than she wanted to handle. Reilly radiated an aura of masculinity that was enough to make a woman swoon. It was no wonder he'd rocketed to superstardom despite the awful films he'd made. There was just something about him, an inner power, an animal magnetism so strong, it no doubt made compasses go haywire. The hairs on her arms were standing on end just thinking about it.

"Don't think about it," she mumbled, breaking in on one mantra with another. "Don't think about it."

Movement. Maybe movement was what she needed to bring her being into proper alignment. She chanted with renewed vigor and volume. She stretched her arms above her head and swung them in a circle, smacking her hand into the side of the bucket full of dirty wash water, knocking it over the edge of the platform she sat on.

The metal bucket managed to hit Reilly a glancing blow off the side of his head before much of the water had sloshed out of it. He dropped to the stage floor like a ton of bricks, his breath leaving him in an unceremonious "Ooof!"

Jayne's eyes snapped open and rounded like saucers at the sound. She stared in horror at the man sprawled below her, face down in a puddle of water.

"Oh, my Lord!" she exclaimed. She scrambled down from her perch just as Faith and Alaina found their way to the stage from the side door.

"Jayne! What did you do to that poor man?" Faith asked, rushing forward.

"It was an accident!" Jayne wailed. She circled the prone figure warily and nibbled at her thumbnail. "What if I've killed him? I was struggling to achieve a sense of spiritual well-being through abstract meditation. It hardly seems right that an innocent bystander should die because of it. Unless, of course, that was his karma," she added on a hopeful note.

Alaina Montgomery-Harrison blew up into her chestnut bangs and planted her elegantly manicured hands at the waist of her brown trousers as she stared at the body. "I hope you're insured. This guy could sue your butt off."

"Spoken with all the compassion of an attorney,"

Jayne scolded, winding her hands into the bottom of her purple T-shirt.

"Sorry, but all my compassion went down the john this morning with my breakfast," Alaina grumbled, slumping down to sit on an overturned crate, careful not to get her alligator wingtips in the dirty water.

Faith kneeled down beside the man on the floor and pressed two fingers to his throat. Her shoulders dropping in relief, she rocked back on the heels of her canvas sneakers and dragged a hand back through her mop of red-gold curls. "I think he's just knocked out."

"Thank heaven," Jayne said, joining her friend on the floor. Her hands were shaking as she tried to push her hair back behind her ears. She hooked the fingers of her right hand beneath her bracelet and slid it around and around her wrist, hoping for a stronger sign of what this all meant, but her source had gone abruptly silent. That in itself seemed a very bad sign. "Do you think I should call an ambulance?"

The man moaned and stirred a bit, his movement rippling the surface of the dirty puddle around him.

"Looks like he's coming around," Alaina commented. "Now, Jayne, whatever you do, *don't* apologize. It's as good as an admission of guilt.

He'll take you for every nickel you've got, and then you won't be able to afford to pay my fee for representing you."

Jayne shot her a look of disgust. Alaina in her normal state was business-minded. Alaina in her newly pregnant state was a shark, a virago, a tigress.

"Ooohhh . . . ," the man moaned.

Jayne pressed her fingers to her pale cheeks and moaned along with him. "Ooohhh . . . I'm so sorry, mister! I didn't mean to crack your skull with that bucket! I'm *so* sorry!"

Alaina rolled her eyes and muttered an expletive.

Jayne leaned down closer to get a better look at her victim. He seemed vaguely, disturbingly familiar, but she couldn't quite place him. She had the distinct feeling she might have known him if his hair had been lighter or if he hadn't had a beard. And there was something about his nose that looked very strange, almost as if it wasn't real.

"Cripes, Jayne, what was in that bucket, battery acid?" Alaina questioned. "This guy's face is coming off."

"What?!"

"She's right," Faith said, frowning. She pulled a packet of baby wipes out of her purse and yanked out half a dozen, which she applied gingerly to the man's face. "I think he's wearing makeup."

"Pervert," Alaina pronounced.

Jayne and Faith rolled the man onto his back, and Jayne's eyes widened impossibly as she stared. The right side of his face had been lying in the water, and his hair on that side had turned blond, the dark color washing out of it to stain the wooden floor. His beard had slid down the side of his face, making him look distorted, like something from a cheap horror movie. Grimacing, she reached out and hesitantly plucked at the limp swatch of fake whiskers. The false beard peeled off and hung from her fingertips like a drowned muskrat.

"Eeeewwww!" she squealed, dropping the dripping mat of hair to the floor.

Alaina sat back and fanned herself with her hand. "Brother, this is getting weird."

"It's just like in *Dawn of the Double Damned,*" Jayne whispered, worried, twisting her suddenly silent bracelet. "That part where Emilio Gustave has turned into one of the pod creatures but Brigette Egbert doesn't know it. And then she realizes it, but it's too late, and he fries her with his eyes and eats her."

"Thank you for sharing that with us," Alaina said sardonically, fanning herself harder as her flawless complexion took on a decidedly green cast.

Jayne bit her lip. "I'm sorry. It was a rotten movie."

Faith continued working with the baby wipes, swiping off a layer of makeup and fake eyebrow. She shrieked in horror when the man's nose suddenly came off in her hand. "Oh, my God!"

"Holy Hannah!"

"AAAAHHHHH!"

"Hey! Wait a minute!" Alaina exclaimed, hauling herself off the crate to get a closer look. "Isn't that? It is! That's no pervert! That's Pat Reilly!"

Reilly moaned again and shook his head in an attempt to clear the clanging bells out of it. Then he opened his eyes and looked directly into the face of Jayne Jordan.

Jayne stared down at him for a long moment, saying nothing. She wasn't capable of speech. She wasn't even aware her two best friends were looking at her expectantly. Reilly's incredible eyes glowed up at her, so blue they were almost startling, so intense she was sure she felt her heart stop just looking at them. Reilly. Her head swam at the implications. He was back, just as he'd promised.

Reilly had returned.

She took one long, hard look at him, all the old hunger and fear rushing to the surface, and fainted dead away.

TWO

"WHAT HAPPENED?" JAYNE asked as she opened her eyes and stared up into Faith's concerned face. "Did I fall asleep? I had the strangest dream. I hope it wasn't an omen."

"It wasn't an o-men, it was *the* man," Alaina whispered, leaning over Jayne's prone form. "The Hunk from Down Under, himself."

"Pat Reilly?" Jayne barely managed to whisper the name. A dozen different emotions all rushed to her throat to choke her. There was dread and traces of a guilt she thought she had rationalized away a long time ago. And underlying that mix of negative feelings was something else altogether. It was like excitement or anticipation or something more primal that she didn't care to give a name to.

Reilly had returned.

"Hello, luv."

The voice was unmistakable. The husky baritone strains reached out like fingers and caressed her skin. Shivers ran up and down the length of her like ribbons rippling in the breeze. Jayne sucked in a horrified breath. This was exactly the way she had reacted to the timbre of his voice the first time she'd met him, when she'd been a very happily married woman. It was a frighteningly automatic response, one she seemed to have no control over whatsoever. It had made her feel wicked at the time. She wasn't the kind of Hollywood wife who bed hopped. She'd been so content with Mac, she had rarely looked at other men to appreciate their male beauty, let alone to contemplate their more hidden charms. So when her husband had brought home the great friend he'd met while on a photographic shoot in Australia, Jayne had been shocked by her reaction, dismayed and disappointed in herself.

She'd loved Joseph MacGregor with her whole being—or so she'd thought. Though Mac had been nearly twenty years her senior, he'd been her soul mate, her anchor and her mentor. She had worshiped and adored him. But on meeting Pat Reilly she'd learned a quick and disheartening lesson: there was a level of attraction she'd never experienced before. To find that out with a man other than Mac had been a crushing blow. It had somehow tainted the love she had for Mac and rippled the surface of the peace she'd found with him.

Now Faith and Alaina leaned away from her, parting like double doors to admit Reilly's countenance to her field of vision, and she was given a refresher course in that lesson. It didn't matter that half his hair was black and half was blond. It didn't matter that his rugged features were slightly irregular—his bold, hooked nose was a tad crooked, his cheekbones were a little too high. It didn't matter that she'd never wanted to be attracted to him. Seeing him now sent her heart into overdrive.

"Bloody hell, I knew you'd be surprised to see me, Calamity Jayne, but I didn't think you'd faint dead away," he said. There was an utterly irresistible smile turning the corners of his mouth, but the bottomless depths of his blue eyes were shadowed with concern as he kneeled down beside her and tucked a finger beneath her chin. "You all right?"

What kind of darn fool question was that? Jayne frowned. Of course she wasn't all right. Her heart was hammering like a washing machine with an unbalanced load. She was alternately hot and cold all over, and her stomach was spinning like a pinwheel in a hurricane.

She pushed herself up on her elbows, sliding back and away from Reilly's touch. "I'm fine."

She was still denying the attraction that pulled between them, Reilly thought. He gave a sharp sigh. She'd always been damn good at that. After her initial unguarded response to him Jayne had more or less pretended he didn't exist except on the silver screen. She had avoided and ignored him to the point that he had begun to wonder if he was the only one who had experienced that searing flame of desire when they'd met.

Just as well, he'd told himself at the time, and he had sought to follow her lead—to ignore his feelings, to direct them elsewhere. He'd even gone so far as to try to cultivate a dislike for Jayne Jordan, dubbing her Calamity Jayne for the havoc her reviews wreaked on movies she didn't like. He'd sent her a pet tarantula as a token of his esteem when she'd panned *Deadly Weapon.* The movie had been a box office smash despite her less than glowing opinion, but still her review had irritated him. And the fact that it had irritated him had irritated him even more. Jayne had been the only movie critic whose opinion had mattered to him.

The attraction had never died. The artificial

dislike had never taken root. And he'd discovered after Mac's death that the desire was still alive inside Jayne as well. She'd merely done a bang-up job of hiding it. She really should have been an actress.

"You could warn a person, you know," Jayne said defensively. She pushed herself to her feet and dusted off her clothes, avoiding a look at Reilly. "You could warn a person instead of just showing up out of the blue, disguised in some kind of weird get up."

Reilly raised an eyebrow as his gaze swept over her from head to toe, lingering on the white socks that bagged around her ankles at the top of her low boots. "There's the pot callin' the kettle black. Anyhow, I did warn you."

Jayne squared her shoulders and stuck her little chin out. "You never did."

He stepped closer, his head bent, rooting Jayne to the spot with his beautiful, powerful eyes. She could not look away from him. Electricity charged the air as his aura invaded hers. It was a moment and a half, Jayne thought. If they'd been filming, this would have been a close up, an instant of silence so full of unspoken emotion, the viewers would have been on the edges of their seats.

"I warned you a year ago, Jaynie," he said, his

voice a low rumble. "I said I'd be back and I'm a man of my word."

"A year is long time," she murmured. "Things change."

"Nothin's changed," he whispered, leaning closer and closer still.

This wasn't quite what he'd planned to do, Reilly thought briefly as he tangled a hand in the wild silk of Jayne's hair. But then he seldom planned anything. He'd always acted on impulse and had never considered changing. He didn't try to resist the force that drew his head down toward Jayne's. And while he could see resistance in her eyes, Jayne succumbed to the force as well.

Her chin tilted upward in a combination of invitation and defiance. If she meant to voice a protest, she never had the chance. Reilly settled his mouth against hers, and Jayne found herself whirled into a vortex of passions that were frightening in their power.

The kiss they'd shared before had hinted at this, but the barrier of MacGregor's spiritual presence between them had ended it. In the time that had passed, Mac's presence had faded, the barrier had thinned, and now the other feelings tore through it like a raging bull through a curtain of silk.

Reilly kissed her deeply, possessively, as if he

had every right. His mouth moved on hers with an expertise that overwhelmed her senses, overpowered any resistance she might have offered. The taste of him was warm and utterly masculine and instantly addictive. She'd learned that a year ago. Kissing him now was like taking a first drink of wine after a year-long abstinence. It was intoxicating, drugging, sapping the strength from her limbs so that she sagged into his arms.

Reilly hauled her up against him with one brawny arm. His other hand remained tangled in her hair, exerting subtle pressure against her skull to alter the angle of the kiss so he would be allowed absolute possession of her mouth. She was every bit as sweet as he remembered. Her body was warm and pliant against his, petite but not without soft curves in all the right places.

If he had wondered over the course of the last year why he couldn't get the taste of her out of his mind, his question was answered now. No other woman tasted quite the way Jayne did. No other woman expressed quite the same mix of emotions in her kiss. With Jayne there was no practiced seduction, no well thought out plot to woo him, no taste of premeditation whatsoever. There was simply pure, unadulterated emotion, and he drank it in greedily.

She reacted to him as automatically as he did to her. As his tongue slid against the warm velvet of hers he couldn't help but wonder what it was going to be like when they finally made love. How could it be anything but explosive? Visions of tangled sheets and hot sweaty bodies wound through his brain. He groaned low in his throat and pulled her tighter against him so he could feel her small breasts flatten against his chest. They were going to be dynamite together—and the sooner the better.

"Well, I guess we'd better be going, huh, Faith?" Alaina said loudly.

Faith cleared her throat nervously. "Yep, I guess we'd better hit the road. We just dropped by to see how you were doing, Jayne."

"And you appear to be doing very well indeed," Alaina said dryly.

Their voices penetrated the sensual fog around Jayne, causing her brain to begin functioning again. Horrified, she pried her mouth from Reilly's and wedged her arms between her body and his, trying to apply enough leverage to free herself from his embrace. He only grinned at her, effectively showing off the cleft in his chin and the boyish dimple in his right cheek.

"Let me go," she demanded, ignoring the primitive thrill racing through her at being his captive.

"For the moment," he said, standing her back from him with a big hand cupping each of her shoulders.

When he let her go, she swayed as if she might swoon again. His kiss had drained all her strength. She shuddered at the thought, then shuddered again as Reilly planted his hands on her shoulders and turned her so she was standing directly in front of him, facing her friends. She made no attempt to escape his hold, sure that if she tried to take even one step on her own, she'd be back down on the floor.

"Don't rush off!" she blurted out, her big dark eyes pleading. The last thing she wanted was to be left alone with Reilly. It was painfully obvious she couldn't trust herself around him, and she didn't trust him any farther than she could throw him. Who knew what would happen if they were left unchaperoned? She got a hot flash just thinking about it.

Faith and Alaina exchanged a significant glance.

"I really have to go, Jayne," Faith said apologetically. "I left Shane watching the baby so I could hit the supermarket. You know he's wonderful with Nicholas, but he's ill-equipped for breast feeding."

Jayne's gaze zoomed in on Alaina's face.

Alaina looked both annoyed and sympathetic, a combination that was natural to her. She was much better at suppressing emotions than expressing them. "Sorry, pal. I've got a will to read at ten. Looks like your moon is in the wrong house."

Not only was her moon in the wrong house, Jayne thought dismally, her planets were all out of alignment as well. Her whole sense of self had been thrown off its axis. She searched frantically for some excuse to get her friends to stay even just a few minutes longer. "You . . . haven't met Reilly yet."

They looked at her expectantly while her brain stalled out.

"Ummm . . . a . . . Alaina, Faith, meet Pat Reilly." She tried to step out of the way, but Reilly held her firmly in place. She shot a glance over her shoulder. His face was unreadable, a polite mask. His hold told her to stay put.

"Reilly is an . . . um . . ." Lord, how did she describe her relationship with Reilly? They weren't precisely old friends, and *acquaintance* seemed woefully thin. He was the man she had been wildly attracted to while she'd been married to one of the most wonderful, kind, understanding men on the face of the planet. Somehow, she couldn't quite bring herself to say that. The burden of guilt was still too heavy for her to confess her sins, even to her best friends. Besides, it would have been a tacky thing to say.

"Reilly is an . . . actor."

Faith gave her a politely puzzled look.

Alaina wasn't so kind. "Oh really? Gee, I thought he looked familiar."

Jayne winced. Crimeny, who wouldn't recognize Pat Reilly? The man was a superstar. Not only was he one of the hottest box office draws in the history of movies, his face was regularly plastered all over the tabloids—usually beside the face of some dazzling starlet. Less than a week had passed since *WE* magazine had decorated their cover with his handsome visage and proclaimed him to be the sexiest man on earth.

Heaving a weary sigh, she pushed past her blunder. "Reilly, these are my friends, Faith Callan and Alaina Montgomery-Harrison." Once again she tried to step aside and once again Reilly's hands bore down on her shoulders. She shot him a glare, but it bounced off his smile.

He nodded pleasantly to Jayne's friends, his jewel-tone eyes sparkling wickedly. "It was a pleasure meetin' you, ladies."

Jayne gasped at his blatant disregard for manners. "Reilly!"

Alaina fought back a grin as she backed toward the exit. "Our cue to leave, Faith. Mr. Reilly, I trust we'll be seeing more of you?"

"Count on it," Reilly said, shooting her a conspiratorial wink.

He took note of the measuring gleam in Alaina's eyes. She was sizing him up to decide whether or not she could trust him with her friend. For the moment she was deciding in his favor; she continued moving toward the door. Faith Callan didn't seem nearly so sure. Her brown eyes were full of worry as she glanced from him to Jayne to Alaina, but she said nothing and continued shuffling reluctantly toward the exit.

It pleased him to know Jayne had such good friends. He had the fanciful feeling they had looked after her in the year he'd stayed away.

"Good-bye," Jayne called forlornly, her stomach sinking.

"G'day!" Reilly called cheerfully.

"Are you going to let go of me now?" Jayne asked as the door closed behind her friends.

"I guess I will," he said, but instead of letting her go he drew her back a step toward him. "I was only trying to protect your delicate feminine sensibilities, you know."

"How so?"

"Well, I didn't figure you'd want your girl-friends to see just how happy I am to see you again." Pulling her back another inch, he wrapped his brawny arms around her waist and eased his hips forward.

"Oh, my goodness!" Jayne said with a gasp. Her eyes rounded like twin full moons. Heat rushed under the surface of her skin. Reilly's rigid manhood pressed into the small of her back. It was all she could do to keep from leaning back into the delicious pressure or, worse still, turning around in the circle of his arms.

Lord have mercy, she was turning into a wanton! Appalled with herself, she bolted forward, breaking free of his loose hold. She pressed her palms to her flaming cheeks and tried to gather together some scrap of composure. She was going to have to be a heck of a lot tougher if she was to survive this visit from Reilly with her heart intact.

Swallowing down the wild fluttering in her throat, she straightened herself and faced him, riv-eting her eyes to the third button on his khaki shirt.

"They might have guessed something from the way you kissed me," she said tartly.

Reilly gave her his patented I-can-see-right-through-your-clothes grin, and said, "And they might have guessed somethin' more from the way you kissed me back."

Jayne narrowed her eyes, peeved. How indelicate of him to point that out. Well, there wasn't a shred of the gentleman in him. She'd always known that. Pat Reilly was rough and rowdy, an Australian version of the great American cowboy. He looked the part, too, she decided as her gaze wandered. He wore a battered leather bomber jacket and a khaki shirt open at the throat. His jeans were faded from repeated washing and wearing rather than trendy chemicals. They were also indiscreetly snug around that part of his anatomy she wasn't supposed to be looking at. She pushed her gaze downward to his beat-up cowboy boots.

"I had a bad feeling this was going to happen," she mumbled, shaking her head. "I've been having the strongest premonitions."

She rubbed her fingers over her bracelet, but felt nothing except fine gold links beneath her fingertips. A certain sense of panic tightened in her chest.

Reilly snorted. "Premonitions my as—"

"Ask anyone," Jayne said defensively. "I have them all the time."

"Superstitious bunk," Reilly scoffed. "I told you I was comin' back, Jaynie. It was only a matter of time." He licked his bottom lip as if savoring the taste of her and grinned. "I'd say I waited just long enough."

"I don't want you to ever kiss me like that again," Jayne announced primly, turning on her heel and marching across the stage to retrieve the bucket she'd bounced off his head.

Reilly chuckled. "Now, don't go sayin' things we both know you don't mean, luv."

Of all the arrogant . . . ! The man was a rampaging chauvinist. Jayne ground her teeth. Somehow, in Reilly those qualities seemed almost endearing. It didn't figure any more than his rugged features adding up to handsomeness did. She scowled at him. His two-tone hair was disheveled into a punk look. Even that was somehow appealing. She was doomed.

"Why the disguise?" she asked, resigning herself to having a conversation with him. The coward in her would have much preferred to run away, but facing him was her karma, that was plain enough.

Reilly made a face of genuine chagrin. "That

bloody article in *WE*. I should have never agreed to it. 'Sexiest Man on Earth.'" He gave another rude snort and jammed his hands at the waistband of his jeans. "What a lotta rubbish. Now I've women trailin' after me everywhere I go, like a pack of rabid dingoes."

Jayne couldn't help but chuckle. He seemed so put out. She would have thought Reilly more than used to having women staring at him—and more than pleased by it. "Oh, you poor man. Women chasing after you. What a horrible fate!"

He wagged a finger at her. "I'm telling you, Jaynie, it ain't funny. Some of those sheilas are cracked. I'm liable to end up like that poor bugger in *Fatal Attraction*."

She knew all about fatal attractions herself, Jayne thought, sobering. "Then maybe you should have gone back to Australia to lay low for a while."

"I couldn't," he said, his neon-blue gaze trapping hers as if in a tractor beam. "The year was up."

He was very good at his craft, Jayne thought, the critic in her trying to detach itself from her emotional self. He knew instinctively just how long to pause between sentences to make the utmost impact. He'd had her giggling just seconds ago, but with that one well-delivered line, he had

her holding her breath and trembling with anticipation. The man was a natural. His movies might
have been horrible, but he was never horrible in
them.

That was one of the things that had always
irked her about Reilly. He had a wealth of talent
and regularly wasted it on scripts that required
nothing of him. He was handsomely paid to look
irresistible and act tough while this abundance of
ability simmered inside him just begging for some
capable director to draw it out. He could have
been great. Instead, he chose to be lazy.

"What are you doing here, Jaynie?"

She pulled out of her musings at the sound of
his voice. He had wandered off and stood with his
hands on his hips, looking at the wall she'd been
washing.

"I helped organize the community theater
group," she said. "I'll be directing our first production, but cleaning up the place comes first.
This theater hasn't been used in years, and it
seemed a shame. The box office proceeds from the
plays will go toward renovation of the building
and to our young artists' program. There are a lot
of talented young people here. They deserve every
chance to develop those talents."

"A worthy cause. What's the play?"

"*A Taste of Starlight*. It's a romantic comedy with lots of emotion—"

"I know it," he said, nodding his approval. "Should draw a good crowd."

"I hope so."

"And this is what you left L.A. for?" he asked, gesturing to their surroundings. "To join charity groups and hide from me?"

She didn't deny the charge. It was true, in part. She had left Hollywood half hoping Pat Reilly would forget about her. But it wasn't the whole truth. She hugged herself and leaned back against the scaffolding, staring out at the dark, empty expanse of seats. "I didn't want to handle Hollywood without Mac. Too many sharks in the water. And losing him made me see how precious time really is. I wanted to spend mine with my friends."

She had continued writing her syndicated column. Once a week she drove down to San Francisco to screen films. But she'd given up her weekly television show, *Critic's Choice*. Her life had taken on a saner tempo. She still kept up on the business and found it was nicer to watch from a distance than to be thrust into the center of the storm.

Being removed from Hollywood let her feel

completely objective. When she'd lived in L.A., there had been a constant stream of people trying to get into her good graces. None of them had wanted a genuine friendship or a real romance. All of them had wanted good reviews.

Good reviews meant big money. A thumbs up from her could make a movie a runaway hit. A thumbs down from her could kill a film before it even got out of the gate. Her friendly, conversational style and her reputation for honesty had won her a tremendous following among the moviegoing public.

"And what are you doing here, Reilly?" she asked. "I thought you'd signed on to do *Road Raider Part III*."

He wouldn't quite meet her eyes when he said, "Yeah, well, the deal . . . fell through."

The truth of the matter was he'd backed out. He was sick of sequels and shoot 'em up action pictures. In his heart of hearts he wanted to do a movie that demanded something of him. But he was terrified of doing just that. What if he took on a part that demanded something of him and he found he had nothing to give?

For months now he'd lived with the horrible, choking fear that one day the whole world was going to figure out that he wasn't really an actor at all, that he was just a jackeroo from a sheep station near Willoughby, Australia. Then Hollywood would send him packing, and he'd have to return to a home where everyone had grown to depend on him for everything.

It seemed one or another of his relatives always had their hand out for something—generally money. And they seemed to think he should feel obligated to dole it out to them willy-nilly just because he had it. He wasn't a brother or a nephew or a cousin anymore. He was a bloody meal ticket, and he knew they would heartily resent it if the money ran out.

Jayne watched the emotions play across his face as Reilly stared down at his boots, and her heart twisted in her chest. He looked vulnerable. He looked troubled. She could sense the turmoil in him, and she wanted to reach out to offer him comfort.

"What happened?" she asked softly, offering him the chance to unburden himself.

He didn't take it. Not that that surprised her. Reilly was stubborn, having come from a place where men were men. It wouldn't be easy for him to open up to a woman. Jayne realized with no small amount of dismay that, if and when the time came, she wanted to be that woman. Feeling that way was just asking for trouble.

"It just fell through, that's all," he said gruffly, setting his granite jaw. He wasn't about to tell Jayne Jordan he was scared. She'd never thought he had any talent to begin with. It had always rankled that he wanted her in spite of her opinion of his abilities, but want her he did.

He lifted his eyes and blasted her with their powerful beam of magnetism. "It's just as well. Now I've got all the time I need to concentrate on you."

Jayne blinked, feeling like a small fragile animal caught in the mesmerizing gaze of a big golden lion. It took every ounce of courage she possessed just to shake her head. "I don't want that, Reilly."

He took a step toward her, a study in leashed power, and bent his head down toward hers. He hooked a big calloused finger under her chin and whispered in a tone of voice that was like steel sheathed in silk, "Well, that's just too damn bad, sheila, because I made a promise and I mean to keep it. The year's up, luv. Now we find out what this thing is that burns between us."

THREE

SHE THOUGHT HE was going to kiss her again. To her shame, she knew a part of her wanted him to kiss her again. But he didn't. He stared down at her a long moment, saying nothing, gauging her response, she supposed. The air around them seemed so highly charged, Jayne thought it was a wonder her hair wasn't standing on end.

This was one of the things that frightened her about Reilly. He had such power, was so overwhelmingly male. There was an intensity in him she couldn't even begin to handle. And then there was the little matter of his reputation. He'd been linked in the tabloids with every starlet from Madonna to Molly Ringwald. If only half the stories were true, he'd had a dozen romances in half as many years. She had seen him herself with a number of different women while she'd been living in L.A.

Actors were notoriously fickle. Jayne had had plenty of first-hand experience with that trait before she'd met Mac. They were generally men whose egos were too fragile to withstand criticism, whose passions changed like the wind. They demanded the undivided attention of their partners, always wanting a captive and enraptured audience, because all of life was a stage to them and they all believed they had the starring role.

Reilly was stubborn and intense and obviously fickle. That seemed a lethal combination to Jayne. His intensity would burn her up while they were together, and when his interest wandered elsewhere, she would be left in the ashes.

"I think this is better left in the past," she said, stepping back from him.

"How can we leave something in the past when it hasn't had the chance to happen yet?"

It was a valid question, but she didn't want to answer it. Some things were just never meant to be, that was all. The Chinese called it *jos*—fate, luck. Maybe it just wasn't *jos* for them to get together. Of course, Reilly wouldn't be receptive to that explanation.

"I came here to start fresh," Jayne said. "I don't want ghosts. I don't want guilt."

Reilly heaved a weary sigh. He'd had this argument with himself more than once in the past few months. He speared a hand back through his bicolored hair impatiently. "Mac's dead, Jaynie. Dead and buried. There's no reason for the livin' to go on feelin' guilty. We shouldn't feel guilty that we're alive and he's not. We shouldn't feel guilty that we want each other." He held up a hand to cut her off when she opened her mouth to protest. "And don't deny that you want me, luv; I know damn well you do."

Jayne bit her tongue on a naughty word. She picked up her bucket again and retrieved the orange sponge that had bounced away.

"Okay," she admitted as she edged backward toward the wings, stage right. "Maybe I do want you. But I'm not interested in being just another in a long line of your paramours, Reilly," she said, shaking her dripping sponge at him. "I'm not interested in having you suck up my whole life like some kind of a human tornado and turn it all inside out and upside down. I'm settled here. I've found a certain amount of existential bliss. I know where the center of the earth is. I don't need you barging in and knocking me off my spiritual axis."

Reilly shook his head as he followed her off-stage and into the cluttered area beyond. There she went, spouting off all that metaphysical garbage again. The woman knew more senseless double-talk than any ten politicians. Whether she realized it or not, she used it like a shield to ward off people. Only the very patient or the very weird were willing to try to get past it. He was neither, but he'd be damned if he was going to let her fend him off with it.

"You can stay on your bloody axis if you like," he said as they went out into the hall backstage. In one graceful move he turned and corralled Jayne against the yellow wall with an arm braced on either side of her. "But I'm not going anywhere, luv. I've lived with wantin' you for too long to call it quits now."

"Ah, so that's it. I'm a challenge to you," Jayne said, trying for some of Alaina's dry sarcasm. The slight quiver of hurt in her voice ruined the effect. She wished she could melt through the rough plaster wall behind her. Hard little nodules bit into her scalp and her back as she pressed against it. "Heaven help me, that's got to be like waving a red flag in front of a bull. Well, you can't have me, Pat Reilly. So there!"

He caught her slender arm as she ducked

under his and started to stomp away from him. "Dammit, Jayne, that's not it and you know it."

She glared up at him, her dark eyes gleaming. "I don't know it," she snapped, losing control of some of the anger she had stored up inside her long ago, anger at being attracted to Reilly, anger at having him be attracted to her. "I was your best friend's wife. What better challenge could there be?"

Reilly swore long and colorfully, fighting for control of his temper. His hand tightened convulsively on Jayne's arm. "I loved Mac like a brother. I never woulda done anythin' to hurt him. But he's dead, goddammit, and we're not. How long are you gonna go on lettin' him protect you, Jaynie? You've got a life to live."

His words went straight to Jayne's heart and stuck there like needle-nosed darts. She pried his fingers from her upper arm one by one and carefully straightened the sleeve of her oversized coat, while struggling to force the tears out of her throat. She needed to get away from him. She couldn't think at all when Reilly was around. His intensity disrupted her spiritual oneness with her intellectual self. The man was a gosh darned nuisance.

"If you'll excuse me," she whispered, her head bent so she wouldn't get caught in the glow of his eyes again. "I have to use the ladies' room."

• • •

What was she going to do, she wondered as she sat on the chipped Formica counter with her knees drawn up and her chin planted on them. Her whole body burned with want of that man. And her soul trembled with fear of him. Was he right? Was she using Mac's ghost as a cloak to protect her from getting on with her life? Or was she just being sensibly cautious?

Reilly's motives were a mystery to her. He'd made it plain that he wanted a relationship, but he hadn't explained why. He'd denied her charge that she was a challenge to him, but she knew she was. He had wanted her when she'd been Mac's wife, but his friendship with Mac had prevented him from pursuing it. Now she was denying him. She was forbidden fruit, which was traditionally more tempting than the kind that could be easily acquired.

There were other possibilities for his persistence as well. Maybe he'd been plagued by the same kind of guilt as she had, and he saw this as his chance to get her out of his system, to exorcise the guilt he'd felt for wanting his best friend's wife.

Oh, fudge, she thought, a long sigh seeping out

of her, life could be so complicated. She leaned back into the corner, forcibly forgetting her problems for a moment and letting her eyes roam around the ladies' room.

The walls were a moldy green color. Or was that real mold over green paint? Yuk. This place needed a real cleaning. Cobwebs hung like dirty lace from the heat ducts in the ceiling. The door on one of the stalls was hanging by one hinge. Another door was missing completely.

It was a shame the townspeople had let the place go like this. Now that they had a theater group, hopefully interest in the building would pick up as well as interest in the arts.

She would be partly responsible for that renewed interest, Jayne thought with a mix of pride and surprise. She'd never been one to take charge of things, but she'd made an effort to get involved when she'd moved to Anastasia. Involvement had seemed important, involvement with the town, with people . . . with Pat Reilly?

Shivers danced through her. She dodged the question and turned so she was on her knees on the counter facing the grubby, smudged mirror that stretched the length of the sink area. She picked her sponge out of her bucket and began methodically wiping it over the glass. Cleaning was very therapeutic. Symbolic too, she thought as she swiped a layer of dust and grime from her reflection.

If only she could wipe away her uncertainty about Reilly as easily.

There had always been something between them, something nameless, something mysterious, something almost . . . mystical. What if it turned out to be something wonderful? Could she really pass up the opportunity to find out?

Could she pass up the chance to let Reilly overwhelm her? Yes.

"I think you missed your callin', luv." His low voice snapped her to attention. "You were obviously meant to be a housekeeper—an infinitely more honorable profession than the one you hold to now, I dare say."

"You would," Jayne said, scowling at his reflection in the mirror. It was no secret Reilly didn't like critics. He'd been very public in his scorn. So what was he doing here?

He had opened the door just enough to stick his head in the room. He had washed off the last of his makeup. His hair had been wetted and rubbed partially dry. The black dye was mostly gone. Now the golden strands stood up in wayward tufts like miniature shocks of wheat. He looked like he'd just come from the shower.

The thought sent molten heat through Jayne's veins. She'd seen enough of his body on the movie screen to know he was some gorgeous example of the male of the species, all thick rippling muscle. She didn't have to try at all to picture him stepping out of a shower stall with crystalline droplets of water clinging to his sun-bronzed skin and nestling in the tawny curls that carpeted his massive chest. She'd seen him just so in *Deadly Encounter*. For nights afterward she'd dreamed that she had been the one to play Michelle Favor's role of the court reporter caught in the middle of a government sting operation headed by Reilly's character, Jack Gibson.

Now he shoved the door open with a brawny shoulder and sauntered in, his boots ringing on the tiled floor. He stuffed his hands into the pockets of his bomber jacket and leaned back against the post of the first stall. The twinkle in his eye was pure wicked mischief. The smile that tugged at the corners of his mouth was all male arrogance, daring her to throw him out.

"This is the *ladies'* room, Reilly," Jayne said, swiping more dirt off the mirror. "You're no lady. You're not even a gentleman."

"That's right, luv. I ain't some limp-wristed dandy who'll let you chase him away with nothin' more than an ugly word or two."

Lazily he pushed himself away from the support and swaggered toward the counter. His grin had a disturbing feline quality to it. Jayne suddenly felt like a very pretty little bird who was suddenly being denied the protection of her cage.

Reilly clamped his big hands on her waist and easily lifted her down from the counter, then turned her to face him. She fully expected him to press his advantage, but he didn't. As if he'd lowered the power with the twist of some invisible knob, his magnetism settled to a comfortably appealing level.

"See here, Jaynie? You can run, but you can't hide," he said teasingly. He lifted a hand to brush a strand of dark auburn hair from her cheek. His thumb strayed ever so slightly to brush the corner of her mouth, and his eyes blazed when she sucked in a surprised breath. For a second he looked tempted to kiss her, but he took a half step back from her instead.

"Look," he said, suddenly uncomfortable. "I can be like a bloody bull in a china shop."

"Yep," Jayne agreed readily, nodding. "You're a bully." She pointed her sponge at him and narrowed her eyes in speculation. "I'll bet you were a first child. I'll bet you're an Aries. I know someone who would love to read your aura."

A lazy smile tilted up the left corner of Reilly's mouth. "Sounds too kinky for me."

"It's not kinky," Jayne explained earnestly, "but it can be a very sensual experience."

"Guess I wouldn't mind havin' you do it, then," he murmured, scratching his head.

Jayne swallowed hard. The way he was staring at her mouth had her feeling a little faint. Talk about a sensual experience. And he wasn't even touching her! Just the power of his gaze had tendrils of sensation unfurling inside her. Her breasts tingled. A honeyed warmth began to glow deep in her belly. Her fingers toyed nervously with the bracelet that was suddenly buzzing again against the fragile skin of her wrist.

She cleared her throat and tried to breathe in enough air to whisper. "I don't have the proper psychic continuity to do it well."

"What the hell," Reilly muttered as something like warm red wine spread through his veins and pooled in his groin. "We'll pretend. I'm good at pretendin'. It's what I do for a living."

And was he pretending now, Jayne wondered. He was a darn good actor. She would be hard pressed to know when he was acting and when he wasn't. That was another reason she'd pretended she didn't want him around. "We all do our share of it, don't we?" she said wistfully.

"Yeah, we do. But I don't want to pretend anymore where you're concerned, Jaynie." He pulled his gaze away from the lush, vulnerable curve of her mouth and focused on the uncertainty in her eyes. "I don't want either of us pretending. I want us to find out just what it is we've been denying all this time. What do you say? Are you game?"

"I'm scared, Reilly."

"Scared of what? Me?"

Yes, she answered inwardly, but it didn't seem a wise thing to admit to him, so she sought other reasons for her fears. "I don't know if I'm ready to try another relationship yet. And I don't want to just leap into one with you. I really hardly know you at all; you were Mac's friend. And I just don't believe in purely sexual relationships. The Hindus teach that sex is one of the lower chakras, down there with all the baser animal needs. I think human relationships should be on a higher spiritual plane, don't you?"

Reilly stared at her for a long moment, his straight brows lowered over his eyes, his square chin tucked defensively. Pure sex had always sounded pretty darn good to him. Who did these Hindu buggers think they were, mucking up a man's social life with all their mystical mumbo jumbo?

It seemed important to Jayne, though. This was a test of sorts, he figured. Could he be patient enough to sort through all that chakra crap, or was he just after a good tumble?

He wanted her, yes. He burned with want of her. He hardly trusted himself to get within an arm's length of her for fear he'd lose control altogether. But this wasn't about just sex. Realistically, he could get sex any time he wanted it with any number of very lovely ladies. But he didn't want them; he wanted Jayne. He wasn't sure where this desire would lead them, but he knew he had to find out.

"Are you saying you want to be *friends* first?" he asked, the word making him flinch a bit. He couldn't honestly say he'd ever had a woman friend before. It didn't seem natural.

Jayne nodded, then watched with interest as Reilly rubbed his chin while he mulled the idea over. She would have bet her best quartz crystal he'd never had a woman for a friend in his life. He was from the old school where a man valued his mates, his dog, and his woman—generally in that order. If he decided to try it and decided he didn't like it, she would be well rid of him when he left. And if he decided to try it and it worked . . . they could have something wonderful. It seemed the safest way to proceed, though she still preferred that he simply leave.

"All right," he said. "We'll be friends first. Get to know each other, then let things follow their natural course." Which would land her in his bed within the week, he reckoned. Sounded good to him, though he wasn't keen on waiting that long.

Jayne nibbled her left thumbnail. Shoot, that had been too easy. There had to be a catch, something she hadn't taken into account. It was at times like these she regretted being right-brain dominant.

Reilly watched her carefully. Apparently she hadn't counted on him being so progressive-minded. She looked wary, hesitant. Maybe he should throw something in to sweeten the deal, a show of good faith, so to speak.

"I'll help you out with the play, as well," he blurted out before he had a chance to consider his impulsive offer.

A cold wave swept over him at the sound of the words in his own ears. Bloody hell! Had he just offered to be in a play? A play was all acting and no action. He couldn't be in a play! There wouldn't be a single car chase or gun battle, no explosions or brawls. He would be forced to really *act*.

Panic in its purest form gelled in his gut. He took a deep breath and willed it away. This was a community theater group not Broadway they were talking about. It wasn't *Macbeth* they were doing, it was a little romantic comedy. The other people in the play wouldn't be actors either—at all, he amended hastily. They would be accountants and supermarket clerks. He could handle this. No sweat. It would be a walk in the park, a piece of cake.

Jayne studied the play of strange emotions that crossed Reilly's face, thinking back to his enigmatic explanation of why he wasn't now in the Mojave Desert shooting *Road Raider Part III*. Once again she caught a glimpse of vulnerability in him, and it touched her. Darn, she had always been one to take in strays. When Reilly's beautiful eyes took on that haunted look—however brief— she wanted to wrap him in her arms and take care of him.

What a lot of hogwash, she told herself as the moment passed and he was suddenly the same old Reilly, cocky and full of himself. She had been imagining things. Reilly needed a caretaker about as much as he needed a third eye.

'You'd really be in my play?" she questioned.

"Sure," he said with a nonchalant shrug, as if he hadn't been sweating bullets over the idea just a second ago.

Jayne hugged herself and sighed. She could ill afford to turn him down. Pat Reilly's name on the marquee would mean a lot of extra money for the theater group and for the young artists. Having Reilly in the play would surely generate interest in the project. People would be eager to get involved and would hopefully stay involved on a long-term basis once they discovered how enjoyable theater was. And this was her chance, wasn't it? This was her chance to do what she'd dreamed of doing since the first time she'd seen Reilly in a little-known Australian film in which he'd had no more than two dozen lines. This was her chance to direct him, to coax out the phenomenal talent she was sure was lurking under his handsome hide.

She nodded slowly, then tipped her chin up and treated him to a sparkling sweet smile. "All right. We'll give it a shot."

Reilly had to fight the sudden urge to give a whoop and do a victory dance. He hadn't realized how important it was to him that Jayne consent to see him. The enormous sense of relief that sluiced through him left him feeling almost giddy.

He gave her a roguish grin that flashed his dimple at her. "Good girl, Jaynie. Now let's go to your place, and I'll get settled in."

"You'll what? Where?" Jayne asked dimly, her head swimming.

Reilly swung the bathroom door open and held it. His expression was as innocent as an altar boy's as he looked back at her. "I can't very well stay at a hotel. The minute word's out I'm stayin' in town, I won't have a moment's peace. Since we're gonna be mates now, I reckoned you'd let me bunk at your place."

"Oh, did you?"

Jayne couldn't help but smile. The stinker! He'd no doubt had that little plan in his head all along. She tried to tell herself deviousness was not an adorable quality, but, somehow, in Reilly it was. At the moment the worst his behavior stirred in her was a deep sympathy for his mother. What that poor woman must have gone through raising Reilly!

"Well, sure," he said, keeping his angelic look firmly in place. Boy, this was going to be good. If they were staying in the same house, there was no way they could go more than a couple of days without succumbing to the sexual attraction that sparked between them. His mouth was literally watering at the memory of the taste of her. His fingers itched to trace over her petite curves.

Jayne gave a shrug of acquiescence, picked up her bucket, and sauntered out the door. "Okay."

Reilly felt as if she'd just smacked him between the eyes with a hammer. "Okay?" he mumbled dazedly. Had she just said okay? He rushed to catch up with her and hovered over her from behind, nearly clipping her heels with his size twelve boots. "Did you just say okay? I can stay at your place?"

"Yes." Jayne beamed a smile up at him, thinking it was kind of fun being sneaky. Then she turned and continued down the hall toward the exit with a spring in her step.

Reilly shot a look heavenward. His heart was hammering in his chest. "Thank you," he whispered, raising his hands in emphatic praise to a benevolent God. "That was almost too bloody easy."

Jayne grinned to herself as she walked ahead of him. "You've got that right, mate."

FOUR

REILLY FOLLOWED JAYNE home, keeping his Jeep a discreet distance behind the red MG—just in case. Jayne's driving was enough to keep a team of guardian angels sweating. Her little sports car wandered from one side of the winding road to the other as Jayne's attention swayed from one point of interest to the next. She nearly clipped a pair of bicyclists while admiring the view of the seashore and just managed to swerve out of the path of a tour bus in the nick of time when a sheep at the side of the road caught her interest. It was enough to give a man a heart attack. Even the Australian sheep dog sitting in Reilly's passenger seat whined in anxiety.

"I know, Rowdy," Reilly mumbled. "She's enough to drive a man bonkers."

Heaven knew she had done it to him, he reflected,

unable to keep his own mind from wandering. Lately Jayne had occupied his thoughts to the exclusion of all else. Now they would find out once and for all if this thing between them was more than passion, more than the lure of the forbidden. Anticipation coiled, warm and tight, low in his belly.

He slowed the Jeep and hit the signal, following Jayne off the coastal highway and onto a private drive that climbed around a hill and cut through a stand of pine trees. The drive eventually widened into a farm yard. Jayne's car skidded to a halt, and she jumped out as if she'd just won a race.

"Here we are," she said with forced cheerfulness. Her heart was in her throat. Inviting Reilly here and having him here were two very different things. The farm was so much a part of her that having him on it seemed strangely intimate to her.

Wondering if she'd done the right thing, she wound two fingers into her bracelet. Nothing happened. No buzzing, no warmth, nothing. She smiled nervously at Reilly, then scowled at the bracelet as Reilly climbed down out of his Jeep. The darn thing was getting mighty selective about its premonitions all of a sudden. Great. Just when she most needed the charm's guidance, the thing had developed some kind of psychic snafu.

She turned her worried gaze to Reilly. There

was a fine layer of dust on his leather jacket, and his golden hair was wind-tossed. He squinted as he looked around, etching lines into the tan skin beside his sky-color eyes. He looked supremely male, rugged and tough, ready to conquer the untamed wilderness and the odd stray female he might find in it. The thought made a little whimper catch in Jayne's throat. Maybe bringing him here hadn't been such a hot idea after all.

"So where's the house?" he asked as his dog jumped to the ground and ran off to explore.

"This is the house." Jayne swung an arm in the general direction of the building and self-consciously tugged at her wild mane with her other hand, thinking she probably looked like the bride of Frankenstein after the drive up the coast in her convertible.

Reilly stared at the large weathered gray building she had indicated and frowned. "Jaynie, that's a barn."

"*Was* a barn," she corrected him. "I had it converted."

"I don't guess I'm surprised by that," he said with a shrug. It was something Jayne would do. Other women in her financial position would have built themselves a palatial estate with manicured lawns and statuary. Jayne lived in the middle of nowhere in a converted barn.

He studied the building more closely, taking note of the large multipaned windows that punctuated one long side. There was half of a whiskey barrel overflowing with dainty purple and white flowers beside the door. On a wooden park bench beside the flowers a black and orange cat was curled up, its tail twitching back and forth as its yellow eyes glared at Reilly's dog. Rowdy gave a sharp bark at the cat and quickly dodged away, loping off across the yard.

Reilly's gaze swept the farmyard, taking in the assortment of other smaller buildings. There was a chicken coop with exotic chickens browsing in the fenced pen around it, brilliant-colored birds with elaborate combs and extravagant tail feathers. Nearer the house stood a small dairy parlor with herbs growing on the sod roof. A large patch of the yard had the beginnings of a vegetable garden sprouting. On the far side of it stood a small stable with a split-rail corral extending beyond. Rowdy stood with his paws on the lowest rail, intently regarding the small herd of shaggy, long-necked llamas on the other side.

A fond smile tugged at the corners of Reilly's mouth. Jayne couldn't have sheep or cows, like anyone else. She had to have llamas and chickens that looked like they were from another planet. She probably didn't even think that was unusual. She was blessed with an innate naïveté he had heretofore encountered only in young children. But Jayne was certainly no little girl, he reminded himself as the lapel of her jacket gapped away and he glimpsed a small, full, unencumbered breast outlined beneath her T-shirt.

She shrugged and looked around her, her wild hair bouncing around her slender shoulders, the dark strands catching fire in the morning light. "What do you think?"

"I like it," he said, his voice low and rough, his gaze glued to Jayne. When she looked up at him like a startled doe, he cleared his throat and gave his attention over to the object of her question. "It's a nice place."

The farm didn't much resemble the sheep station he'd grown up on and had thought to spend his life working, but it gave Reilly a sense of home, just the same. It was a simple place. It was a place where a man could smell the earth and feel the clean air on his skin. It was a far cry from L.A. It suited Jayne. And it suited him, he decided.

"How much land have you got?"

"Four hundred acres. It's mostly wilderness. I always wanted a farm," she rambled on, poking her nose into the open back of Reilly's Jeep to see if there was anything she could carry. "I don't mean to farm it, though. I don't take to all that machinery."

She grabbed the handle of an enormous duffel bag and wrestled with it until Reilly gently shooed her aside. He lifted out the battered bag as if it weighed nothing and slung the strap over his broad shoulder. Jayne looked up at him and swallowed hard. He was standing much too close. The twinkle in his eyes and the quirk of his lips made her breath catch.

"I've always believed having lots of natural open space around frees a person to become spiritually in touch with the primordial planes of pure existence." She swallowed hard. "Don't you think so?"

"Grew up on a farm, didn't you?" Reilly said, ignoring her mystical prattle.

"Yes. My daddy was a barn manager at one of the big thoroughbred farms in Kentucky. Paris, Kentucky. I always used to pretend it was Paris, France, but—"

"Jaynie?" he questioned softly, his azure eyes dancing. Moving no more than half a step, he had her trapped between his body and the side of the Jeep. "Are you nervous about havin' me stay in your house?" His voice dropped a velvety octave to a tone that made all Jayne's nerve endings hum. "What's the matter? Don't think you can trust yourself with me sleepin' in the next bedroom?"

She hadn't actually allowed herself to think that far ahead. Now that he had raised the question, the scene sprang to life in Jayne's fertile imagination: Reilly stretched out, naked, the white sheet tangled around his slim, tan hips, moonlight spilling through the big window and across the bed. All the air seeped out of her lungs in a slow hissing sigh. She was suddenly much too warm inside her clothes.

"We could skip the preliminaries, you know," he whispered, leaning closer. "I don't have any objections to us gettin' to know each other in bed."

Jayne licked her lips and said nothing. It was really quite frightening how badly she wanted him to kiss her. She had to make a concerted effort to keep the heels of her low boots on the ground instead of raising them up until she was on tiptoes, straining to get her lips closer to his.

The sudden slam of the screen door jolted her as if it had struck her.

"Did you get my Fig Newtons? I'm just gonna *die* if you forgot them again, Jayne," a distinctly feminine voice with an East Coast accent whined.

Reilly jerked around to glare at the source of the voice, and his mouth dropped open in sheer shock. Standing at the door of Jayne's house was a girl of about sixteen wearing ragged jeans and a black T-shirt with the logo of a heavy metal band emblazoned across the front. She wore her orange and black hair in a crown of spikes that resembled the headdress of an exotic lizard. She had a safety pin dangling from the lobe of one ear, and she was very, *very* pregnant. She stared back at him with kohl-ringed eyes that grew wider and wider and wider.

Jayne used the moment of silence to compose herself. She stepped away from Reilly's Jeep—and Reilly—straightening her oversized jacket and re-capturing some of her sense of inner calm. She wasn't going to be alone in the house with Reilly. Far from it. She concentrated on the sense of relief that ran over her and ignored the disappointment.

"Ohmygod! Ohmygod!" the girl mumbled in-coherently, pressing her hands to her pale cheeks. Her fingernails were painted black. "It's—it's—ohmygod!"

Jayne shook her head and cast a wry look at Reilly. "If you could bottle your effect on women and sell it, you'd be able to call Donald Trump poor white trash."

Reilly scowled at the remark but didn't take his eyes off the awe-struck punk creature advancing on him. He took a wary step backward.

"Candi, heel," Jayne said, catching her young charge by the shoulder, halting her pursuit of Reilly, who was plastered against the side of his Jeep. "Candi, this is Pat Reilly. He was a good friend of my late husband. He's going to be staying with us for a little while."

Her description of their relationship didn't escape Reilly, and he shot Jayne a cold look. She was trying to put a barrier between them, trying to resurrect Mac's ghost. Well, it damn well wouldn't work. He opened his mouth to tell her so, but her next words brought him up short.

"Reilly, this is Candi Kane. She's living with me until she has her baby."

"She's what?" he croaked as all his hot visions of bedtime games were thoroughly dowsed with the cold water of reality.

Jayne's lips curved slowly upward in an incredibly smug smile. "Candi lives here. With me. In my house. Twenty-four hours a day."

Reilly planted one hand on his hip and rubbed the other across his jaw, caught between equally strong urges to laugh and to wring Jayne's pretty neck. He gave in to the first and quelled the second. The little minx! No wonder she'd given in so easily to his request for housing. His broad shoulders shook as he wagged a finger at her. "Don't think you've got the better of me, sheila."

Jayne sniffed. "I didn't know there was a better of you."

"It all looks choice to me," Candi whispered reverently, her eyes eating Reilly up.

Jayne shot her a scorching look. "It's talk like that that gave you an expanding waistline, young lady."

"Jayne!" the girl wailed, mortified. Her face flushed a furious shade of red. She lowered her voice to an embarrassed hiss. "Jeeze, did you have to bring *that* up?"

Jayne rolled her eyes. "Honey, I don't think it escaped his attention. Reilly's not naïve enough to think you were just hiding a medicine ball under your blouse." Her hands cupping Candi's shoulders, she gave the girl a serious once-over. "Now, how are you feeling today? You don't look in imminent danger of death from lack of Fig Newtons. Good thing, too, 'cause I forgot to get groceries."

"Again?" Candi shook her spikey head and cast a woeful glance Reilly's way, apparently having survived being star struck. "I hope you didn't come here for the food. What little there is, is weird. Just wait until you get a taste of her tea." She made a face that more than described her opinion of the brew.

Jayne took umbrage at the slam against her cooking. "I grow the herbs for that tea myself. And, I'll have you know, my all-natural cuisine is very healthful."

Candi snorted. "Sprouts and oat gook. A person could starve."

"You eat like a marine!" Jayne argued, throwing her hands up in disbelief.

Candi tugged on the bottom of her T-shirt and stuck her nose in the air, presenting them with her ample profile. "Well, I *am* eating for two."

"Who? Arnold Schwarzenegger and Refrigerator Perry?"

The girl ignored Jayne and looked at Reilly hopefully. "Can you do anything besides look devastating? Like cook?"

He chuckled. "I can fry steak and eggs with the best of them."

She sighed heavenward. "Maybe there is a God, after all. Now, if you two will excuse me, I have to go get prone; my feet are swelling. Nice meeting you, Reilly."

"*Mr.* Reilly," Jayne corrected her with a dire look.

"Whatever."

Reilly dropped a hand on Jayne's shoulder and stood beside her, watching in silence as Candi waddled back into the barn-cum-house. "Did her folks really name her Candi Kane?"

"Yep."

"Crikey, they were askin' for it."

"And they got it, too." Jayne shook her head. "She's a handful."

"How'd she end up with you? Sounds like she's from New York or someplace like that."

"Providence, Rhode Island. She's a runaway," Jayne explained. "I sort of adopted her from a shelter in San Francisco. A friend of mine is a counselor there. He introduced me to Candi, and I just kind of brought her home with me.

"She's a good kid, really," she said, appealing to Reilly with her liquid black eyes. "She's just made a lot of bad choices. She could have a very bright future if she'd quit trying to sabotage herself."

Reilly lifted a hand to brush his fingertips along the curve of Jayne's cheek. "Trying to save the world, Jaynie?" he asked softly. There was no sarcasm in his voice, no derision, but a kind of sweet curiosity. His eyes glowed with it.

"Just a little piece of it," Jayne replied honestly, her lush mouth turning up at one corner in an endearing smile.

As much as he had wanted to have her all to himself, Reilly couldn't find it in him to be angry or even annoyed at the presence of Candi Kane. Looking down into Jayne's sweet face, all he could feel was a strange warmth in his chest. It was something like pride, only more intimate, something that seemed very special, very rare.

"You're one in a million, Calamity Jayne," he murmured.

And he leaned down and kissed her—not in the possessive, sexual way he had kissed her before. This kiss was gentle, a benediction. Jayne drank in his approval. She felt as if the sun had come down and encircled her with a golden glow.

When he lifted his head, Reilly tweaked her nose and gave her a wink, nodding in the direction of the converted cow barn. "Come on, luv, show me to my stall."

Jayne loved her house. She had designed it with two things in mind—comfort and open spaces. One room flowed into the next with scarcely a wall in the place. One bonus she hadn't even considered at the time was the lack of privacy. It was going to be very difficult for Pat Reilly to get her totally alone in a room . . . or for her to get him alone, she added with a frown.

Her common sense might have been wary of Reilly and his motives for wanting to rekindle the previously forbidden flame, but her hormones were all for jumping into the nearest bed with him, Jayne admitted to herself. It seemed she was no more immune to Reilly's roguish charm than the rest of the women on the planet were.

Who was she kidding? She had no immunity to it whatsoever. If she had, she would never have given him a second look when Mac had introduced her to him all those years ago. The temptation to betray her beloved husband would never have crossed her mind or blackened her conscience.

Mac's dead, Jaynie. Dead and buried. There's no reason for the livin' to go on feelin' guilty.

But guilt was only a part of the bigger picture.

Reilly stood with his hands planted at the waist of his jeans, staring off across the sweeping expanse of the first floor with something like disbelief in his eyes. He'd never seen anything quite like it. The living areas were divided by various groups of furniture or by curtains of hanging plants. There were heavy posts and beams aplenty, but there was nary a solid wall on this level.

They walked through an enormous kitchen where copper and iron pots and bunches of dried herbs and flowers hung from the heavy ceiling beams, and where a polished, pine harvest table dominated the floor space. The cupboards had been constructed of weathered barn siding. The cobalt-blue tiled counter tops were crowded with Kentucky salt-glazed pottery.

Beyond the kitchen, on the north side of the building and up three steps, was a more formal dining area. On the south side and down three steps was a sprawling living room with plush lavender carpet. The south wall was virtually all window, decorated by nothing more than a deep purple velvet swag valance artfully slung on a thick brass rod.

The collection of furniture in the room could only be called eclectic. Bon Jovi blared from a tall French armoire crammed with stereo equipment. A low, black-and-gold japanned trunk topped with a thick slab of glass served as a coffee table. It was cluttered with old books and magazines. There were iron floor lamps with fringed shades and a bamboo cage made in the likeness of an elaborate house with two tiny birds flitting about within it—no doubt trying to escape the rock music, Reilly thought.

For lounging there were three huge, ornate Victorian sofas upholstered in purple brocade. Two were piled with paisley-print pillows in shades of mauve and purple and green. One was occupied by Candi, sprawling the length of it with her stocking feet propped on one arm and her spikey hair sticking up over the other. She was thoroughly engrossed in the latest copy of *WE* magazine.

Reilly scowled at the picture of himself staring out from the cover of the magazine with a crooked grin. Turning away, he nearly plowed into an aquarium. He pulled himself up short and stared in utter disbelief at the contents of the tank.

"Bloody hell! That's a tarantula!"

"I know," Jayne said calmly, as if everyone she knew kept one. "You shouldn't be so surprised. After all, you sent him to me."

Reilly opened his mouth and clamped it back shut. He looked from Jayne to the huge hairy arachnid and back again. He had bought the thing at a pet shop and sent it to her when she'd panned *Deadly Weapon*. It had been a practical joke, just one of many he had played on her over the years. "I never expected you to keep it!"

Jayne leaned over the tank and crumbled in some homemade spider food, smiling as Harry scrambled over a rock to get to the treat. She turned an angelic look up to Reilly. "What else could I have done with him?"

For the life of him, he couldn't think of a single thing to say. He couldn't name one other woman of his acquaintance who would have kept a tarantula.

"I voted we sent it to that big roach motel in the sky," Candi said. "That thing gives me the creeps. No offense intended, Reilly."

"None taken," he mumbled, shaking his head.

"And you shouldn't let that ugly thing keep you from asking Jayne out. She's not *that* attached to it."

Jayne reached over the back of the couch to pluck the magazine from Candi's hands. "This doesn't even remotely resemble an algebra book."

Candi ignored the hint. Struggling into a sitting position she kept her eyes on Reilly, who had wandered off to inspect a Chinese screen. "Jayne, do you have any idea who he is?" she said in a conspiratorial whisper. She snapped a finger against the magazine cover. "He's the sexiest man in the universe. You've got the sexiest man in the universe in your living room, and you're showing him your pet spider. What's the matter with you?"

"Nothing. Are there any helpful articles in this magazine? Like one that advises people to mind their own business?" Jayne asked pointedly. It hadn't occurred to her that Candi would want her to pursue Reilly. She had thought the girl would act as a buffer, just like her younger sisters always had when she'd been a teenager bringing boyfriends around.

"No," Candi said, "but there's plenty in here about what a stud this guy is."

Jayne scowled, not appreciating the reminder in the least. If it was at all possible, she was going to try to think of Reilly in asexual terms for the time being.

She would try to think of him as a fellow life force in her circle of existence, a spiritual energy, a hunk and a half. Oh, fudge, she thought, grinding her teeth.

"Don't let the glitter get in your eyes, sugar," she advised Candi sagely as she handed her the magazine. "He's just a man."

Candi gave her a long-suffering look that suggested she thought Jayne a bit dim. "Jayne, my uncle Fred who sells orthopedic shoes is just a man. That fat guy that comes to read the meter is just a man. Pat Reilly is *awesome*."

She was right, Jayne thought with a sinking heart as she stared across the room, meeting Reilly's smoldering gaze. Everything inside her turned to warm honey. There were men and then there was Reilly. There was definitely something about him that set him apart—an inner fire, a blazing sexuality, a bod to die for. And she now had to accompany that something to a bedroom.

Offering a fervent little prayer to every deity she could think of, she crossed the room and motioned for him to follow her. The trip up the winding open staircase to the second floor seemed to last an eternity. She could feel Reilly's gaze on her derriere every step of the way. She was so aware of it, it was like a tangible caress. By the time they gained the second-story landing, her breathing was labored and her knees were weak.

Practicality had dictated there be at least a few walls in this part of the house. There were four spacious guest rooms, and Jayne's own large suite, which was set apart from the other bedrooms by a lofted den. She flung open the door to Reilly's room and turned to him with a skittish smile.

"Here you go. All the comforts of home. You even have your own bath." She sidled toward the steps, shooing him toward the room with an airy wave of her hand. "Go on ahead. Settle in. Settle away. I'll just—"

Reilly took a step backward and propped himself against the wall, effectively cutting off Jayne's escape route. A lazy smile twitched his lips. "Aren't you gonna give me the grand tour, Jaynie? What kind of a hostess are you?"

Jayne's brows drew together in annoyance, and she crossed her arms tightly against her chest, not realizing that she was plumping her breasts up practically under Reilly's nose. Her black eyes sparkled. "It's a bedroom, Reilly. I hardly think you, of all people, need a map."

That was an argument best left alone, Reilly decided. His love life had been blown out of all proportion by the Hollywood press, but he did certainly know his way around a bedroom. To his way of thinking, a man didn't discuss such things, particularly with a lady and most especially not with a lady who had qualms about becoming just another notch on his belt.

"Come on, Jaynie," he said in his most persuasive tone. He gave her a little-boy's smile that was designed to melt the coldest female heart. "How are we supposed to get to know each other if you keep running away from me?"

Her eyes narrowed dangerously, and she took a deep breath in preparation for delivering a scathing retort, but Reilly cut her off. He pried one of her arms free and tugged her into the bedroom after him. "You can keep me company while I settle in. We'll have a nice chat."

Three feet into the room she dug her heels into the plush slate-gray carpet, and Reilly reluctantly let her go. She chose to stand next to the large oak bureau, well away from the king size bed. Just seeing Reilly standing by the thing was suggestive enough to make her pulse race.

"I like your house," he said. He plopped his duffel bag down on the ruby-red woven bedspread. With efficient movements he unzipped the bag and began unpacking, laying his things out in neat stacks—shirts, jeans, socks, underwear. "It's kinda strange, but it suits you."

"Gee, thanks," Jayne said dryly.

Her gaze wandered over his belongings, lingering on his briefs. They were plain, serviceable white cotton. No fancy designer labels for Reilly. The sudden image of him in nothing but a pair of white skivvies seemed to Jayne like one of the sexiest scenes ever to cross her imagination. Heat swept over her. Unfortunately, none of it came from her left wrist, where she was compulsively twisting her bracelet around and around in hopes of some kind of a message.

"Any other surprises I should know about?" he asked, shooting her a glance over his shoulder.

"Surprises?" she parroted absently, her attention riveted on the wayward strands of golden hair falling across his forehead. Her fingers itched to brush them back.

"A pregnant teenager, a herd of llamas, a tarantula in the livin' room. These are not things the ordinary person has around, luv. Anything else come to mind?"

"I can't think of anything out of the ordinary."

"Now, that's a comfort." He chuckled to himself. "Oh, except Bryan."

Reilly went utterly still. Every muscle in his body tensed. He stood at rigid attention, his intense gaze pinning Jayne to the spot. His voice was deceptively, dangerously soft. "Bryan? Bryan who?"

"Bryan Hennessy."

A dozen thoughts rushed through Reilly's head. He was too late. Some bugger named Bryan had snuck in and snatched Jayne out from under his nose. He would beat the blighter to a bloody pulp. Then he'd give Jayne a good shaking because she'd known he was coming back. He'd promised, and Pat Reilly never broke a promise; everyone who knew him at all knew that.

Jayne could sense the jealousy in him. She could see it seething in the depths of his fathomless blue eyes. She could feel the negative energy radiating from him. A little shiver of primitive excitement went through her. He'd never looked bigger or more aggressively male than he did at this instant, and Jayne couldn't control her instinctive response. She didn't like it, but she understood it. On the most basic male-female level, she wanted to be Pat Reilly's woman. It was hardly a comforting thought.

"He's staying in the old dairy parlor," she said. "He's a friend."

Reilly closed the distance between them with two slow strides. He looked down at Jayne but resisted the urge to touch her. "Like I'm a friend?"

"No." It occurred to Jayne that she could have

been stubborn about this. Reilly had no legal claim on her. He had no right to act possessive and get all macho and jealous. But it seemed important to clarify this point right now. These were two men who were very important to her for very different reasons. She didn't want any misunderstandings about that. "Bryan recently lost his wife. He's staying here because he needs to be near his friends right now. He's like a brother to me."

Some of the tension eased out of Reilly's broad shoulders. He wouldn't feel entirely at ease until he'd met this Bryan character for himself, but he believed Jayne had no romantic designs on the fellow. She wasn't the type to lie, nor was she the type to try to make a man jealous. Jayne would never indulge in catty little games. She didn't possess that kind of female guile.

He gave her a sheepish smile, embarrassed at the way he'd behaved. He was coming on with all the finesse of a steamroller. "Like a brother, eh? Well, that's okay then, I guess. I don't reckon we'll step on each other's toes, seein' how what I feel for you ain't brotherly in the least."

Jayne tried to ignore the wave of warmth that swept down her body along with Reilly's heated gaze. "Oh, thanks for your permission, Reilly," she said sardonically. "You can't know what it means to me."

He chuckled at the feisty look she was giving him. Damn, but she was cute. "You're welcome, luv," he said with a grin, dimple flashing. "Ask for it any time you like."

Jayne nearly choked on the urge to scream and laugh at him at once. She shook a tiny fist under his nose instead, unsuccessfully fighting back a grin. "Darn you, Reilly. You tempt me to say a very naughty word."

"Really?" he questioned, one golden brow sketching upward. There was a thoroughly wicked gleam in his eye as his hand closed around her slender wrist. "You tempt me to act out five or six I can think of."

He knew he shouldn't do it, but when he got this close to Jayne, when he touched her, what little caution he possessed vanished. When he touched her, desire flared through him unchecked. All he could think of was wanting her and having her and how damn good it was going to be. Control was like a word from a foreign language, and discretion sounded even stranger.

"Lord, you do tempt me, Jaynie," he murmured, his warm breath fanning the soft skin of her hand as he raised it to his lips.

Keeping her gaze locked with his, he slowly brushed his lips across her knuckles. Pure male satisfaction thrummed through him as he gauged her response. Her eyes darkened to purest black. Her ripe, moist lips parted slightly, invitingly, and he doubted she was even aware of the small sound of yearning that escaped them. He was very aware of it; it pierced his chest and burned a path to his groin.

Feeling reckless, he drew his mouth across her knuckles again, this time letting his tongue ride slowly over each ridge and valley. Jayne went pale. Beneath her purple T-shirt her small firm breasts rose and fell, nipples straining against the fabric.

"Stop it," she whispered, nearly incapable of speech. Fear rippled through her. What was she going to do? She was losing herself. She could feel Reilly's awesome power taking her over. That he could wield so much control over her with so simple an act was terrifying. She couldn't handle this kind of intensity.

Reilly could feel her pulling away from him emotionally. He could sense her fear. He was in danger of crossing a line he had promised Jayne he wouldn't cross. No matter how badly he wanted to, he wouldn't take the seduction any further. That final step would have to be hers, or he would lose her. That prospect was not acceptable.

Immediately he toned down his overwhelming sexuality, leashed his desire. He gave Jayne a gentle smile. Turning her hand over, he pressed a sweet kiss to the fragile skin of her wrist and nuzzled the unusual gold bracelet she wore.

"What's this, Jaynie?" he asked, fingering the delicate charm that dangled from the chain, wondering dimly why it seemed to turn so warm against his skin. "The key to your heart?"

Something like that, Jayne thought. Reilly, whose psyche was well grounded in mundane reality, wasn't liable to understand about the bracelet. She decided not even to try to explain the power that small piece of gold held. The only person who truly understood it was the person who had given it to her—Bryan.

"Maybe it's the key to my heart," Reilly murmured. The sincerity in his gaze made her breath catch. She didn't resist as he drew her hand to his chest and flattened her palm over his heart. Even through his khaki shirt she could feel his warmth, the hardness of his pectoral muscles, the steady thud of his heart.

"Thanks for lettin' me stay, Jaynie," he said softly. "You won't regret it. I promise."

He leaned down, intending to drop a quick kiss on her lips, but froze when Candi appeared in the doorway with a knowing smile on her face.

"A—hem," she said.

Jayne bolted back away from Reilly, blushing guiltily. Pat just grinned and chuckled, utterly unrepentant.

Candi snickered. "Pardon me, Jayne, but your palmist is here."

"Oh. Fine." Jayne rubbed her hand against her belly as if trying to erase the incriminating evidence of Reilly's touch. She didn't even attempt to meet his eyes as she scooted toward the door. "I'll let you get settled in then, Reilly."

"Right," he said, eyes twinkling as he winked at the teenager.

In the hall Jayne shot a stern look at Candi's smug expression. "There wasn't anything going on, you hear?"

"Oh, I'm sure." Candi laughed sarcastically. "Jayne, it's okay if you've got the hots for the guy. I mean, you're thirty-something, and he's the sexiest man in the universe. Go for it."

"He's just a friend."

The girl rolled her kohl-ringed eyes and nodded, her black-and-orange spikes bobbing. "Uh-huh."

Reilly lounged in the doorway to his room, his broad shoulder propped against the doorjamb, his arms crossed over his chest. He smiled to himself as he watched Jayne and her pregnant punk descend the stairs.

"Just a friend?" he murmured. "We'll see about that, Jaynie."

FIVE

"Pat Reilly's here. He came, just like he said he would," Jayne said. She nibbled on her thumbnail and looked to the one friend she had confided in about her attraction to Reilly, the one friend she had always confided in.

Bryan Hennessy sat on a stack of hay bales in the llama barn, his brow furrowed in concentration as he held a dollar bill out in front of him. His big hands moving with surprising grace, he made the bill disappear, then tried to bring it back. What appeared in his hand was a dilapidated silk daisy with a bent stem. He frowned.

"That's eleven dollars I've lost. I'm going to go broke on that trick," he muttered to himself.

"Bryan, did you hear me?" Jayne asked, losing her patience.

"What? Who?" Bryan pushed his glasses up on his nose and regarded Jayne with solemn, serious eyes as he tucked the daisy into his shirt pocket. "Reilly's here, did you say? Hmm. . . . Do you want him here?"

The word *no* teetered on the tip of her tongue, but didn't quite spill out. It wouldn't have been the absolute truth, and Bryan would have known that. Even in his current state of emotional pain, he could read her with uncanny ease. Jayne had long ago accepted the fact that she and Bryan were kin on a spiritual plane that transcended ordinary relationships. She seldom questioned or fought against anything highly spiritual. There was no point to it. A person's karma was a person's karma, after all.

"I don't know what I want," she admitted, almost wincing as conflicting emotions clashed inside her.

She bit her lip and wound her bracelet around her wrist. Bryan leaned his back against a thick post. She often found him in the barn trying to regain his lost talent for magic tricks or just sitting and staring at the llamas. He seemed to have lost all interest in his work as a psychic investigator, even though he was in demand all over the world as a renowned expert on ghosts and other such phenomena. It tore Jayne's heart out to see him suffering, but she knew from experience he needed time to grieve over his wife's death.

Bryan had come to Anastasia from Scotland two months after his wife Serena's death, needing the support of his friends. They had given it to him without question or reserve over the past few weeks. Jayne had given him use of her dairy parlor, which she had converted into a guest house, so he would have privacy but be near enough for her to keep an eye on. It seemed ironic that now she was coming to him for advice and support.

She had slipped out of the house as soon as her palmist, Wanda Styles, had gone. Wanda had been no help at all, pointing out a winding, wobbly love line on her hand and predicting she would need to invest in an exotic, scented, edible body lotion. And Candi, whom Jayne had planned to use as a buffer to keep Reilly at bay, had been suggesting all kinds of ways for Jayne to snag the man. It had been downright unnerving to hear the girl's schemes—especially once she realized her brain was giving them a certain amount of consideration.

Jayne braced her arms on the rail of the stall before her and stared unseeing at Mascara, a black-and-white female llama with unbelievably long lashes fringing her gentle brown eyes. The llama reached her long neck over the stall, begging for a scratching, which Jayne provided automatically as her thoughts turned back to her friends.

The Fearsome Foursome had ended up in Anastasia, just as they'd planned all those years ago. Each had gone off to chase a rainbow, a rainbow that had shattered or lead down the wrong road or simply faded away. Now here they were, all living in the town they had chosen as a refuge of sorts. Faith and Alaina had found new lives here. Each had achieved her ultimate dream of fulfillment. Bryan was simply hanging on, trying to survive a family tragedy. And Jayne, Jayne mused, Jayne had been in a holding pattern . . . waiting for Reilly's return.

As if her imagination had conjured him up, he walked into the barn, stopping just inside the door. His face was an unreadable mask as his gaze drifted from Jayne to the man sitting on the hay. "Am I interrupting?"

"Not at all," Bryan said, pushing himself to his feet. He was every bit as tall as Reilly. Not as brawny, but equally athletic-looking, Jayne noticed. She didn't miss the intensity in either pair of blue eyes as the men regarded each other. Bryan was the first to offer his hand. "Bryan Hennessy. You must be Pat Reilly."

"I am."

As they shook hands, Jayne watched Bryan's face. The hint of a smile lifted one corner of his mouth.

"Jaynie," Reilly said, not taking his eyes off the man before him, "you've got a phone call from the editor of the *San Francisco Chronicle*."

"Oh. Thanks," Jayne mumbled, nibbling on her thumbnail as her gaze darted back and forth between the two men. It settled on Bryan, and he looked at her, giving an almost imperceptible shrug. Jayne's eyes widened.

What do you mean, you don't know? You always know.

Not this time, sweetheart.

Reilly frowned at the pair and the silent communication obviously going on between them. His scowl only darkened when Bryan reached out and gently tapped a forefinger against the little gold key that dangled from Jayne's wrist. Jealousy burned through him. He'd always been a tad bit territorial, but with Jayne he felt downright primitive. He was sick of having to watch other men share her affections. He'd had no say in the matter when she'd been married to Mac, but damned if he was going to let this buck move in to challenge him now.

"Shake a leg, sheila," he snapped at Jayne. "It's a toll call."

Jayne gave him a strange look but hurried out just the same.

The instant she was out of earshot, Reilly wrapped a fist in Bryan Hennessy's shirt front and leaned toward him, the picture of male intimidation. "You lay a finger on her, and I'll break it off and feed it to you for breakfast. You got that, mate?"

Bryan had the gall to look mildly amused. He removed Reilly's hand from his shirt with deceptive calm. "We're clear on that, but maybe I should explain something to you. Jayne is like a sister to me. I wouldn't hurt her any more than I would stand by and watch some outback Casanova break her heart. You got that, *mate?*" His voice was low and calm, but the threat was implicit.

Reilly grinned suddenly. With the danger of a rivalry removed, he liked this Hennessy—a man who stood his ground and spoke his mind. He gave Bryan a brotherly thump on the shoulder. "We're square then."

"Be careful with her," Bryan said, his expression dead serious. "Jayne is very special."

"Don't I know it," Reilly murmured, his gaze straying out the door just as Jayne emerged from the house wearing an enormous straw hat with pink silk cabbage roses on it. She had changed into a shirtwaist with a long, flowing, flowered skirt, and she towed a recalcitrant Candi Kane behind her as she marched toward her car. The teenager was protesting loudly about going to her doctor's appointment, but Jayne wasn't having any of it. Reilly smiled fondly. "Don't I know it."

The cast of *A Taste of Starlight* sat in the auditorium seats of the community theater staring past their director with their mouths hanging open. Jayne tried to ignore the feeling that she was talking to a group of zombies and pressed on with her explanation of why the sexiest man in the universe was joining their ranks.

"Mr. Reilly is an old friend who has agreed to appear in the play as a favor," she said. Not one of them blinked or in any way acknowledged her. They went on staring at Reilly as if mesmerized. "As I'm sure y'all realize, his participation will boost our attendance considerably, boosting our box office receipts as well, adding badly needed money to the coffers of both the community theater and the young artists' program. I know I speak for all of us," she said with a touch of irony, "when I say we greatly appreciate his generosity with his time."

They didn't move an inch.

"I know I can count on y'all to keep Mr. Reilly's participation our little secret, too. It's our duty to protect his privacy while he's here."

There wasn't so much as a flicker of awareness in response to her statement. They might have been mannequins for the amount of animation they displayed.

Candi, who sat at Jayne's right with her red high-top sneakers propped up on the seat in front of her, glanced up from her article on natural childbirth and gave the amateur actors a disgusted look. Having easily forgotten her own star-struck reaction to meeting Reilly three days before, she said dryly, "They'd make a terrific mime troop."

Jayne gave her a silencing look, then glanced back at Reilly who stood slightly behind her. He seemed distinctly uneasy. The expression in his eyes was almost wary. He had twisted the script she'd given him into a cylinder of dog-eared pages. Now that she thought about it, he hadn't said a dozen words on the drive to the theater.

As she looked at him, trying to puzzle through the clues of his mood, the vague image of the conversation they'd had the morning of his arrival came back to her. He'd looked the same way while evading her questions about why he wasn't filming *Road Raider Part III*. She had sensed the same kind of tension in him during that conversation. How odd.

He couldn't possibly be nervous about doing the play, she thought. Reilly uncertain of himself? When pigs fly. He was a veteran actor with a dozen major motion pictures under his belt. He had worked with some of the biggest names in Hollywood. He couldn't possibly be having qualms about appearing in a little community theater production.

Still, that was the feeling she was getting, and Jayne had always been wise enough to trust her feelings, her clues as to how others behaved and reacted. She had built her career on trusting those highly sensitive instincts.

She reached out automatically for Reilly's hand, needing to offer him support more than she needed to avoid contact with him. She'd been watching him warily for three days now, studiously avoiding touching him—a tremendous feat for a woman who found touching as normal and essential as breathing. Truly, it was a tremendous feat for any woman living in the same house with Reilly.

After the scene in his bedroom that first morning, she had braced herself for an all-out assault of her senses. But he had behaved himself admirably. With the notable exception of having taken over her kitchen, he had been a polite and courteous house guest. For that Jayne was appreciative, relieved, and depressed all at once.

But this was not the time to mull over the contrary swing of her hormones. She drew Reilly a step closer to her so he was standing beside her and gave him a gentle, reassuring smile. "Let me introduce you to everyone before we get started."

Reilly listened intently as Jayne went through the row of volunteers, trying to channel his panic attack into something positive, like a good memory. The heroine of the play, a nightclub singer named Desiree Angel, was to be played by Cybill Huntley, a slightly plump CPA with a glazed look in her green eyes and silvery blond ringlets that fell to her shoulders. One of Desiree's matchmaking aunts was to be played by Jayne's palmist, Wanda Styles, a woman who bore a startling resemblance to Elvira of horror movie fame. She was dressed all in black and wore half a pound of eye makeup. The other aunt was to be played by Marlene Desidarian, an extra-large legal secretary in an orange tie-dyed T-shirt who wore an armful of copper bracelets. Phil Potts, the county clerk, was taking on the role of the nightclub manager. Phil was forty-five and balding with a little Hitler moustache and a pleasant smile. The club's bouncer was to be played by Arnie Von Bluecher, a giant with a German accent who designed and made jewelry and sold it in his own shop in Anastasia's marina area.

These people were going to look to him for inspiration, Reilly thought. They were going to expect him to act up a storm. They were depending on him to help them pull this show off. What if he couldn't do it? What if he let them down? His performance was no less important to these people than his participation in *Deadly Intent* had been to his director friend who had invested heavily in the picture and was on the brink of bankruptcy. They were counting on him the same way his cousin Mick was counting on him to back his charter airline business.

Suddenly his broad shoulders seemed braced against the weight of the world. He broke out in a cold sweat. The instinct for fight or flight was urging him to turn tail and run, but he wouldn't do that. Pride kept his booted feet rooted to the floor. Pride and a decade's worth of old chewing gum. The theater's floor had yet to receive the benefits of a good cleaning.

Jayne glanced up at him with a question in her eyes. He answered it with a decisive nod. He had promised her he'd help her. Damned if he was going to let a little blind panic stop him.

She went on with her introductions, finishing up with the stage manager in charge of curtains and props, Timothy Fieldman, a seventeen-year-old nerd with taped-together glasses and calf eyes for Candi Kane. Candi was to be their makeup artist.

"Do you think that's wise?" Reilly asked under his breath. He took note of Candi's bruise-blue blush as the girl turned her spikey head to bat her lashes at Timothy. "Or did I miss somethin' here? Is this the *Nightmare on Elm Street* version of the play?"

"Don't worry," Jayne assured him, patting his arm. "She'll do just fine. Besides, you'll look great with spiked hair."

He started to protest, then caught the twinkle in her eye and chuckled instead. He knew he was in trouble when Jayne could put one over on him. His sense of humor was in sorry shape. He blamed it on a lack of sex, something he hoped to rectify soon. He was about fed up with the getting acquainted stage of their relationship. He honestly couldn't see why one activity had to preclude the other, but that was the way Jayne claimed she wanted it.

To his way of thinking, they had gotten to know each other the moment Mac had introduced them. In that instant they had been as starkly aware of each other as two creatures could be. Perhaps what she meant was for them to start fresh, without the barrier of Mac between them. And so they had. But enough was enough.

He watched the naturally seductive sway of Jayne's hips beneath her dark paisley skirt as she walked toward the stage, and heat coursed through him like a river at flood tide. He acknowledged that he was more than ready to chuck this half-assed wait-and-see plan she'd formulated and get on to the important stuff.

The first night of practice wasn't going to amount to anything more than a read-through of the script, but Jayne had decided to make the occasion a special launching of their project. She'd spent much of the afternoon with her cleanup crew finishing work on the stage. They had even managed to set up some of the props for the first scene.

Now she nodded to Timothy as a signal for him to go open the heavy old curtains—a flourish signifying the beginning of their theatrical endeavor. He didn't budge. His gaze was on Candi.

"Timothy?"

"How do you get your hair to stay that way?"

"Spray starch." Candi smiled at him sweetly and patted a hand to her crown of unmoving spikes.

"Wow. That's so cool."

"Timothy?" Jayne asked again, more forcefully. "The curtains?"

His head snapped around as if she'd jabbed him with a cattle prod. "Oh, gosh! Oh, gee! I'm sorry, Miss Jordan! I'm really much more diligent than this. You'll see."

He scrambled up out of his seat in a tangle of gangly arms and legs and fell all over himself in an effort to appear highly efficient. When he finally made it to the stage and pulled on the rope to open the curtains, nothing happened. He pulled again. Still nothing. On the third try, he jumped off the ground and yanked on the rope with all his meager might. The curtains separated all of three feet before tearing from their hooks and collapsing to the stage in a dusty, moldy heap of age-rotted fabric.

Timothy ran down to the front row of seats, glasses askew. Clumsily he tried to brush the thick layer of dust from Jayne's head and shoulders. "Oh! Oh! Gee, Miss Jordan, I'm really, really sorry." The apology spewed out of him a mile a minute in between gasps, his voice cracking on every third word. "I never meant to break any-thing. I was just trying to do my job the way you told me to. I only want to be efficient. I only want to help. I—"

Jayne halted him, holding him at bay with a straight arm, her hand pressed to his bony shoul-der. "Timothy, it's okay. It wasn't your fault." She looked up at the stage and the sea of red brocade spilling across it, her shoulders slumping. "I guess we'll just have to put new curtains at the head of our list for ways to spend our box office money."

She turned back to her troupe with a sigh. "Come on, gang. Let's take our positions on stage and read through Act One."

For the first time since they'd laid eyes on their illustrious co-star, the group moved. The spell was broken. Chatting among themselves, they left their seats and moved down the aisle, with only

Cybill still staring at Reilly as if he were an alien being. They all clambered onto the stage, stepping over and around the fallen drapery, eager to examine the set.

The first scene took place in Desiree's one-room apartment, where the only significant piece of furniture was an ornate brass bed.

"Nice choice of props, boss," Reilly said, his low voice washing over Jayne in an intimate wave of warm sensation. He stuck his hands in his jacket pockets and leaned down to whisper in her ear. "What say we try it out later?"

Jayne felt her cheeks grow hot. Excitement jumped to life inside her and collided with a heavy wall of apprehension. Three days had hardly been long enough to discern what Reilly's intentions were. How long *would* be long enough, she wondered. She'd had no luck trying to read his mind, and she was getting no help from her usual source of premonitions. She was flying blind and she didn't like it any more than she liked Reilly's sudden change in tactics.

Darn the man. She had never been able to maintain her equilibrium around him. That blasted animal magnetism of his made her personal field of life energy go haywire. If he had any idea how badly he rattled her she would be lost.

Perversely, a part of her thrilled at the prospect of being lost—lost in Reilly's arms. She shivered.

A stream of patented Pat Reilly curses snapped her out of her trance. Jayne looked up to see Reilly backed against a wall, being confronted by a determined-looking Marlene, who probably outweighed him by twenty pounds. While Wanda and Phil looked on with interest, Marlene made a great show of fluttering her eyelashes and moaning as she began running her hands all around Reilly's head and shoulders, almost but not quite touching him.

Jayne burst out laughing as Pat looked to her with an expression caught somewhere between shock and desperation.

"You've got one hell of an aura, studmuffin," Marlene said in a gravelly voice as she stepped back from him, her dimpled hands falling to her sides, bracelets rattling. "I'll bet you're a Leo with Pisces rising."

Reilly wore an expression of outrage. "It's none of your bloody business what's risin'."

Marlene ignored his outburst and turned toward Jayne with a shrewd expression. "You've got your hands full, honey."

"Don't remind me," Jayne grumbled.

"I'd love to read your palm sometime," Wanda

said in a husky voice, reaching out toward Reilly's hand. She had inch-long blood-red nails and a ring shaped like a spider.

Wide-eyed, Reilly squeezed away from the wall and dodged Wanda and Marlene. He grabbed Jayne by the arm and dragged her a few feet away, all the while keeping a wary eye on his attackers. Marlene looked like an upright freezer with a fading blond braid. He'd seen less formidable foes in tag-team wrestling matches. And Wanda was enough to give Vincent Price the shivers.

"Reilly, I like having *two* arms," Jayne protested, squirming in his grasp.

He loosened his hold, but didn't let go. His eyes blazed like sapphires. His square jaw jutted forward aggressively, showing off the cleft in his chin. "Everyone in this bloody town is cracked. That's it, ain't it? Psychics and palmists. Everythin' here is turned around back to front and upside down. It's just like in that movie where all them wives turned out to be witches, ain't it?"

"Oh, calm down," Jayne said. She smoothed her hands down the arms of his jacket, subtly aware of the hard muscled strength beneath the battered leather. "Marlene didn't hurt you. She was just reading your aura. I told you it was a very sensual experience."

"Superstitious rot," he grumbled. "Scared the bloody bejeepers out of me, she did."

He straightened his broad shoulders, tugging down the waistband of his jacket as if resettling the cloak of his dignity. Indignant, he gave Jayne a sideways look. "She touched my aura. Here I was, savin' myself for you. Now I feel cheap and tawdry."

He was putting her on. The realization struck Jayne with a burst of good humor and a touch of uneasiness. He'd shifted gears so smoothly, she hadn't even noticed.

She gave him a look and called out, "Places, everyone! We're going to walk through the first act. That's called blocking. I want you to follow your scripts, read your lines on cue, and move where I tell you to move. Don't worry about doing it perfectly." She smiled beguilingly at her amateur actors. "Remember the main reason we're here—to have fun!"

Cybill, who had the lead role, not only forgot to have fun, she forgot how to speak. The woman opened her mouth for her first line and nothing came out but a mouselike squeak. After the third try, she turned to Jayne, purple with embarrassment, tears pooling in her eyes, and murmured, "I guess I'm a little nervous."

"Honey, there's nothing to be nervous about," Jayne assured her, patting her arm. She didn't miss Cybill's furtive glances at Reilly, who was lounging offstage since his first appearance in the story didn't happen until midway through the first act. A pang of sympathy ran through her. She certainly knew what it was to lose all sense in Reilly's presence. Poor Cybill had been literally struck dumb by the mere sight of the superstar.

Reilly seemed to understand it as well. He pushed himself out of his chair, crossed the stage, took Cybill by the arm, and led her a couple of steps toward stage left. Jayne thought the woman looked ready to faint dead away, but Reilly appeared unconcerned.

"Everybody gets nerves from time to time, luv," he said gently, smiling down indulgently into her adoring gaze. "All you have to do is remember how simple this is. You get cast for a part, you read the lines, do what the director says. It's simple." He gave her a conspiratorial wink and nodded toward Jayne. "Mind you, don't let the boss know how simple it is. She's liable to replace us with trained monkeys."

Cybill's frigid fear dissolved into nervous giggles.

Jayne felt her heart melt into a gooey puddle in her chest. How sweet of Reilly to set Cybill's self-conscious fears aside. Most of the actors she'd known were too wrapped up in their own insecurities to worry about anyone else's.

She thanked him with a private little look as he sauntered by on his way back to the wings. He slowed his stride just enough to murmur, "Thank me later," in a black satin whisper. Fanning herself with her script, Jayne turned back to the actors onstage.

This time when Cybill opened her mouth, her line came out. It was wavy and warbly, but the next one was better, and the one after that was pretty good. The first scene proceeded without a hitch. Midway through the second scene Reilly made his first appearance.

It was worse than an E. F. Hutton commercial, Jayne thought. The only sound was the distant clank of the building's ancient heating system. Every eye in the place was glued to Reilly—Reilly, who suddenly looked a little pale beneath his tan. She watched him closely herself, but for very different reasons from those of the rest of the cast and crew.

Something was wrong. She could feel it. She could sense it in the way he moved. His fluid, athletic grace had fled. A muscle twitched in his jaw.

He plowed through his first nine lines with all the finesse of a bear dancing in high heels.

No one else seemed to notice his lack of grace and style, probably because their own performances were devoid of either quality. But they were amateurs in their first play. Jayne didn't expect them to be anything other than awkward. Reilly, on the other hand, was a world-class talent, and she was a world-class critic.

"Let's take a coffee break, everybody," she said as Reilly ended the act on a note that, to Jayne, was as flat as an anvil. She almost winced when he delivered it. "There's coffee and cookies backstage."

As the others gravitated toward the coffee maker, Jayne pulled Reilly aside. "Is something wrong?"

Nerves gelled into a lump in his stomach. She'd seen it. She'd found him out. He should have known this would happen. If anyone could spot him for a no-talent phony, Jayne could. He must have been temporarily insane to volunteer to be in a play she was directing.

"What?" he asked defensively, suddenly angry with her for her oft-stated opinion of his meager talent. He felt an instinctive need to lash out, and Jayne was destined to get the brunt of it. She was the root of all his problems—the object of his desire had been his best friend's wife, a woman now bent on keeping a distance between them, a woman now directing this bloody play. "What? I didn't dazzle you? As if I ever could."

"What's that supposed to mean?"

"Don't expect anything more here than you see on the screen, Jayne."

Jayne felt as if she'd just walked in on the middle of a foreign film; nothing he was saying made any sense to her. "I just thought you seemed a little tense, that's all."

A gross understatement if ever there was one, she thought. Reilly looked like a human time bomb about to go off. He loomed over her, the tension vibrating in the air around him.

He spoke from between clenched teeth. "Lack of sex. Care to do anything about that, sheila?"

Jayne scowled at him, crossing her arms over the front of her plum-colored sweater. Her booted toe tapped impatiently against the worn wooden floor of the stage. "You blame everything on a lack of sex. I swear, if you went bald overnight, you'd blame it on a lack of sex."

"Yeah, and it'd be true. I would'a torn it all out by the roots."

"Well, maybe you should channel some of that

pent-up energy into your acting, because what you're giving me here is flat," she said, hoping to goad him into performing.

Her strategy worked a little too well. Reilly hooked an arm around the small of her back and hauled her up against his body. Her eyes widened at the feel of him as her hips pressed against his.

"Luv," he said on a growl, his mouth just inches from hers, "believe me, what I want to give you is definitely not flat."

"You are an absolute vulgarian." Her words were as stiff as her body in his arms as she fought the urge to melt against him.

"I'm a man, Jaynie. A man has needs . . . just like a woman does. Tell me you don't need it, Jaynie," he demanded softly, his tone of voice a lesson in seduction. Of its own volition his free hand came up to comb her wild hair back from the delicate line of her cheek. "Tell me you haven't lain in bed every night for the past year aching for it the way I have."

He could tell by the flare of desire in her eyes she had. Her body betrayed her if her words didn't. The longing was there in those obsidian depths, just beneath surprise. "Yeah, I've waited that long, Jaynie," he admitted. "I'll warn you—I'm not inclined to wait much longer."

The fine trembling that coursed through her was an intoxicating mix of fear and anticipation. Jayne stared up at him with doe eyes, the coward in her wishing she could be anywhere else in the universe. But along with the fear and the anticipation was a dark sense of inevitability. She couldn't be anywhere else in the universe because what had begun between her and Pat Reilly while she'd been MacGregor's wife was far from over.

The noisy return of the cast broke the spell that had wound around them. Reilly released her and strode away. Without a word to anyone he headed for the coffeepot with his hands in his pockets, hoping to disguise his state of burgeoning arousal.

The plan to woo Jayne slowly was shot to hell now, but then he'd never been much for plans anyhow. His impulsiveness just now had gotten more of a reaction out of Jayne than three days of playing the gentleman had. They were never going to find out anything about what could be between them if they went about this Jayne's way, he reflected as he poured himself a cup of coffee and added gagging doses of sugar and cream.

She was trying to protect herself, he thought as he absently chose a cookie and nibbled on it. He could understand that. He could understand it, but he damn well wasn't going to allow her to do it.

Jayne resumed her role of director, congratulating herself on a stellar performance. Inwardly, she was a jumble of raw emotions and painful doubts. Outwardly, she appeared to be confident and cheerful, if a little subdued. Ignoring Reilly's uninspired performance, she took her amateur thespians through Act Two with quiet competence. All went well enough until they reached the pivotal scene between the heroine, Desiree Angel, and her hero, Wilson Mycroft.

It was the first really emotional scene between the two lead characters, the first scene where they actually touched each other. They took their places, standing beside the brass bed. Reilly put his arm around Cybill's shoulders, keeping a discreet distance between them. Knowing what was in store, Cybill took one look up into Reilly's famous blue eyes and went mute again. Jayne frowned and nibbled on her thumbnail, at a loss as to how to handle the situation.

"She's not exactly Meryl Streep, is she?" Candi murmured. She stood beside Jayne, one hand braced against her aching back, one rubbing her protruding belly. "I'd volunteer to take the part, but I don't think I could get close enough to him."

Jayne gave her a wry look. "I'm afraid you wouldn't be very believable as a virginal ingenue."

"No," Candi said with a snort. "But at least I can talk."

"Jayne, I can't do this," Cybill whispered, her voice trembling with desperation. She had abandoned Reilly and now grabbed onto Jayne's arm with a death grip. "That's Pat Reilly. The script says I'm supposed to *kiss* Pat Reilly!"

Jayne heaved a sigh. "Cybill, honey, he's just a man."

Cybill was astonished. "Jayne, are you out of your mind? Rodney Povich at the hardware store is just a man. My husband is just a man." She jerked her thumb in Reilly's direction. "That's *Pat Reilly.*"

Jayne's shoulders drooped in defeat. Candi gave her an I-told-you-so look.

"Why don't you walk through it with me, Jaynie," Reilly suggested, his tone thick with dangerous undercurrents. "Show Cybill what a snap it is."

Jayne glared at him. He was being obnoxious in the extreme. She was beginning to regret her dream come true of directing him. He'd been subtly difficult ever since his first scene. He wasn't giving her even a small sampling of the talent she knew he possessed, the talent she had been so determined to bring out. If anything, he seemed to be fighting it—fighting her—and she was darn near ready to give him a swift kick in the seat of his well-worn, indecently snug jeans.

"All right," she said tightly, picking up her script as if it were a gauntlet he'd thrown down.

She took her place before him, standing beside the, fancy brass bed. He pulled her much too close and looked down at her, his eyes blazing with challenge and belligerence and barely leashed passion. A strange recklessness tilted her chin up, and her mahogany-fire hair spilled down her slender back and over Reilly's arm.

"Put a little something into it this time," she suggested beneath her breath.

"Oh, I'd be glad to, luv," he muttered, his eyes flashing at her unintentional double entendre.

"Wilson," Jayne began, thankful she had memorized most of the play, since she couldn't pull her eyes away from Reilly long enough to read her lines, "how am I supposed to quit this life? I need the money. If I leave Lucky Louie's now, Aunt Mabel and Aunt Catonia will lose their home. They'll be thrown out in the street."

"I'll help you, Desiree," Reilly said stiffly.

"How can you help? You dress up in a chicken suit and pass out handbills on the sidewalk. Don't tell me—that's just a hobby. You're really the third-wealthiest man in America."

"No, I'm not. But I'd be the richest man in the world if only I could have your love, Desiree."

As directed in the script, Reilly gazed down into Jayne's eyes and the earth shifted suddenly beneath his feet. His anger vaporized, slipped through his grasp like smoke. The tension that had had him in its grip since his first line of the evening melted. Awareness of his surroundings dimmed. His focus was wholly on Jayne, on the feel of her in his arms, on the way the light turned her hair to a nimbus of dark garnet around her head.

This was what he wanted. This was what he had craved for so long—to hold her in his arms like this. When she was this close, his heart pounded in a rhythm he didn't recognize, and his head filled with cotton wool. She was so pretty, so feminine with the wide ivory lace collar of her sweater framing her slender shoulders. And there wasn't a reason in the world she couldn't be his.

"I'd have everything a man could want if I had your love," he murmured, his words sweet with longing and wishing. "I'd be everything I'd ever hoped to be with you by my side."

Dazed and dazzled, Jayne stared up at him, barely aware that they were on stage. Breathlessly she recited her next line, her heart skipping erratically in her breast. "Tell me you love me."

"I love you," he said hoarsely. The script dropped from his free hand and fell to the floor unheeded. He speared his fingers into Jayne's hair, his big hands framing her face, and lowered his mouth to hers.

Jayne sighed and leaned into him. It was a sweet kiss, full of hunger and hesitancy, and she drank it in as if she hadn't been kissed in years.

The cast broke into wild applause, cheering and whistling.

Reilly lifted his head, his eyes cloudy with confusion. Jayne reacted more quickly, bolting out of his arms, scrubbing at her flaming cheeks.

"That was wonderful!" Cybill exclaimed, her eyes brimming with tears as she came forward to congratulate Jayne on her performance. "But I'll tell you something, Jayne. If he kisses me that way, I promise you I'll have an aneurysm and die."

That didn't seem like an altogether bad idea, Jayne thought. She was trembling all over as if she had severe malaria. Fever and chills chased each other over her skin. She felt as if her bones had all dissolved. One kiss and her sense of self had shattered like a supernova.

And for Reilly it had all been an act.

SIX

HE'D PUSHED TOO hard.

Jayne, who usually rambled on nonstop, her conversation flowing from one topic to the next, had been virtually silent on the drive home from play practice. Candi had filled the awkward quiet with her wry observations about the cast, about the way rehearsal had gone, about Timothy Fieldman, who she thought was kind of cute in a nerdish sort of way.

Reilly hadn't had much to say. He'd been too caught up in memories of the way Jayne had felt in his arms during the scene they had played together, of the way the whole world had disappeared and every ounce of his energy had been concentrated on Jayne. More than once during the past year he had wondered if what he'd felt that day at Mac's graveside had been a figment of his imagination. It hadn't been. He'd felt it again tonight.

They were on the verge of something special, he and Jaynie. He could feel it in his gut. He only hoped he hadn't blown it by taking the bit in his teeth earlier in the evening. Yes, Jayne had responded to his bullying. She had also sought the refuge of her bedroom the instant they walked into the house.

Reilly didn't waste time wishing he'd been born with the capacity for self-restraint. Nor did he waste time regretting what he'd done. He did waste a considerable amount of time sitting on the sofa in Jayne's den, staring at her closed bedroom door.

Not that he had anything better to do. It was two-ten in the morning. Everyone and everything on the farm was asleep, including Rowdy and the llamas. Even the tarantula was dead to the world. But Pat Reilly was wide awake, suffering through yet another bout of the insomnia that had plagued him for months now. He hadn't even bothered going to bed. He knew he'd be lucky to get two or three hours of sleep, and those wouldn't come for a while yet.

The turmoil of self-doubt that lay beneath his veneer of macho self-confidence always seemed to simmer a little hotter during the night when there was no escaping it. The idea of distracting himself in a woman's arms had crossed his mind more than once, but the one and only woman he wanted hadn't been available to him. Tonight she was within his reach, but a wall stood between them—an emotional wall that could prove to be much trickier to get around than the wooden one that surrounded her bedroom door.

Needing to move and stretch the muscles that coiled with tension, Reilly hauled himself to his feet and began to prowl the den.

It was a comfortable, rustic place with rough planking covering the north and east walls. The room had been divided from the guest quarters by elevating it, giving it a loft effect. A large, soft, white U-shaped sectional sofa invited a person to sprawl out to listen to music or perhaps to watch a movie on the big-screen television. Most of the east wall was taken up with shelving and a cluttered desk area. As with the first level, the south wall was one enormous window.

The view tonight was nothing but a weird combination of moonlight and fog. It made Jayne's big barn house seem cozy and warm, the only solid, safe place to be in a world that had mysteriously evaporated into mist. Once again Reilly had the sensation of being at home. His family's station wasn't often enveloped in a bank of fog, but there was ever the feeling of being in a pocket of security surrounded by wilderness. It was a good feeling, a safe feeling, one he eagerly embraced now, during the long night when there was no one he needed to impress with his sensible self-reliance.

Not wanting to think another thought about this horrible weakness that was afflicting him, he climbed the four steps leading up to Jayne's office area and began to poke around, searching for things of interest. He inspected the desk that was littered with notes, mail, old copies of *Variety*. It never occurred to him to feel guilty about snooping. He wanted to know more about Jayne, so he looked.

There was a half-finished review in the typewriter, waiting for the final touches before she would submit it for her column. He read it over, wincing at the concise manner in which she had cut the film to shreds. It seemed a paradox to him that Jayne, who was one of the most compassionate people he'd ever known, could be so brutal in her critique of someone else's work. Knowing her personality, one might have expected her to be kind and sympathetic toward a bad performance or an unfortunate choice of scripts. Instead, she was painfully honest in her opinions, padding nothing with kind words that could have been misconstrued as praise when she felt none was due.

What Jayne did for a living bothered Reilly much more than her penchant for palmists and paranormal phenomena. The people in the film industry worked long, hard hours to put a movie together. They put heart and soul into their work. It just didn't seem right to him that a critic should be able to sit in supreme judgment like some kind of Grand Inquisitor, able to make or break a picture according to her whim. It just didn't seem democratic. He wondered how big a fight he'd have on his hands if he tried to talk her into quitting.

Mac had been able to live with Jayne's profession, Reilly reminded himself as his gaze fell on a photograph of his old friend. The picture in its ornate, silver filigree frame stood on the shelf above the typewriter. Mac stared out at him with wise dark eyes and a crooked smile, looking enough like Sean Connery to make feminine hearts flutter despite his age.

They had been best friends, he and Mac, but they had been very different from each other. Mac had been calm and pragmatic. Those words were noticeably absent in descriptions of Reilly. It stood to reason his relationship with Jayne would be very different from her relationship with Mac. He wondered now if that idea frightened her. Jayne liked security. She tended to back away from anything that threatened to overwhelm her.

Mulling that thought over, Reilly examined the photo that sat next to Mac's. It was of Jayne, two other young women, and Bryan Hennessy, all in graduation caps and gowns with a rainbow staining the sky behind them. Moving on to take a look at the stuff crammed onto her shelves, he let the subject slide from his mind. He let his gaze drift over a collection of books on theology and mythology. A copy of the *Kama Sutra* caught his eye, and a grin tugged at his mouth as he wondered just how closely Jayne had studied the classic Hindu text on love-making. Lord knew, he was dying to find out.

Another shelf was stacked with books on the film industry, books on screen writing, and on directing and cinematography. He pulled out one of the texts on screenwriting and a sheaf of papers that had been tucked inside the cover dropped to the desk. Curious, he picked it up and read the cover.

"*Everlasting* by Jayne Jordan," he mumbled, his brows lifting in surprise.

It was a script, a screenplay Jayne had written. Before he had a chance to turn back the cover, the bedroom door to his right opened, and Jayne poked her head out. She was hugging her robe around her petite frame. It looked like silk and was black with splashes of fuchsia, purple, and emerald in the form of tropical flowers. She looked sleep-rumpled and wonderfully sexy with her cheeks rosy and her wild mane of dark auburn hair mussed around her head and shoulders. A surge of desire seared Reilly's veins as he looked at her.

"What are you doing up?" she asked, her voice soft and smokey. It was almost like a caress to Reilly's already-aroused nerve endings. He had to clear his throat before he could answer her.

"Couldn't sleep," he said. He gave a nonchalant shrug of his massive shoulders as if to say he didn't find it all that unusual to be prowling around someone else's house in the dead of night.

Jayne didn't fall for the offhand manner. She caught the subtly mutinous set of his jaw that dared her to challenge his casual attitude. Wisely, she chose not to. Reilly would sooner have had his tongue cut out than admit to a woman that something was bothering him. Silly, macho Australian man. Oddly enough, his reluctance to confide in her just brought out her nurturing instincts all the more. She wanted to help him. She wanted to hold him and soothe away his worries, whatever they were.

She wanted to do a darn sight more than mother him, she admitted. He looked impossibly sexy standing there beside her desk wearing gray sweatpants and an old black T-shirt that strained to span his shoulders. His golden hair fell across his forehead in a fashion that hinted strongly at numerous finger combings. The lean planes of his cheeks were already darkening with the shadow of his morning beard.

He was every woman's dream of a rough, maverick male who needed a woman's gentling touch to domesticate him. That look had sold a lot of movie tickets and captured a lot of hearts. Hers was no exception, Jayne admitted with equal doses of resignation and reservation.

When they had returned from rehearsal she had sought the solace of her bedroom, hoping to sort through the complicated maze of feelings Reilly inspired in her, but she'd come to no conclusions as to what to do about him. Now she felt like a kitten that had exhausted itself chasing its own tail—dizzy and confused, no farther ahead than when she'd started.

"Did I wake you?" he asked quietly.

"No. I wasn't sleeping either." For the first time her gaze fell on the papers in his hand and she laughed in delighted surprise. "Where did you find that?"

"Stuck inside one of your books."

Smiling fondly, Jayne moved to stand beside him, her small hands lifting the script away from him. "I'd lost all track of this," she said, her fingers brushing across the cover. "I tried to sell it when I first moved to L.A., but of course I couldn't find anyone who would even look at it."

"You wanted to be a screenwriter back then?"

She gave him an enchanting smile. "I wanted to set the film world on fire as a writer-director. But, like most people who go to Hollywood seeking fame and fortune, I ended up waiting tables. When I was offered the chance to do movie reviews for a local TV station, I jumped at it." She shrugged, her dark eyes twinkling with memories. "The rest, as they say, is history."

"You never tried selling another script?"

"No," she murmured, absently paging through *Everlasting,* not really seeing the neatly typed pages, but thinking of the rainbow she had followed to Hollywood and how it had somehow just faded away. Holding the long-forgotten script in her hands now brought back the memory of it with a bittersweet pang. "My life took a different direction. I suppose it was my karma all along."

"Bunk," Reilly muttered on a snort as he moved on to examine her shelf of videocassettes. It was lined with movies, old and new, movies that ranged from *Casablanca* to *Gone with the Wind*, *The Big Easy* to *Bull Durham*.

"You like being a critic, do you?" he asked, sneaking a hard look at her out of the corner of his eye.

"Yes. I feel like I'm doing the public a service."

"Imposing your opinion on them, you mean," he grumbled.

Jayne frowned at him. "I help people make decisions on how to spend their free time and their entertainment money, both of which most people consider too important to waste on worthless movies."

He intended to turn and level a scowl at her, but a title on the shelf caught his eye, and he did a double take. "Speaking of your idea of worthless movies, what are these doing here?"

Jayne blushed as if he'd just stumbled across a secret stash of porno flicks. She watched as he ran his index finger over the spine of each protective jacket and read aloud the titles of the films that had catapulted him to the stratosphere of superstardom.

"You've got every movie I've ever been in," Reilly said, his disbelief more than evident in his voice. "What the hell is this, Jayne? You hated these films."

"I didn't hate *Outback*," she said defensively.

"I hardly had any lines in *Outback*! That was my first."

"I know," Jayne mumbled. She busied her hands straightening things on her desk, keeping her head down. She was embarrassed to have Reilly discover her secret obsession with his work. It was like having him read her diary or look through her lingerie drawer or find a stack of love letters she'd written but never sent. Still, the cat was out of the bag now. "You were wonderful in it, lines or no."

"I was—" He stopped dead and stared at her as if he needed to translate her words in his head before he could understand them. Then his scowl darkened even more. He jammed his hands on his hips. "The hell I was."

"You were," Jayne insisted. She knew the movie scene by scene. It wasn't a classic. Nevertheless Reilly had stood out like a diamond among rough stones. His natural talent had been obvious and Jayne had been captivated. Her frustration with him had stemmed from his failure in subsequent roles to tap into that talent, a waste that broke her heart as a lover of fine acting.

Reilly shook an accusatory finger at her. "You

trashed every one of these films in your column. You hated them and you hated me in them."

"I did not!"

"Oh? Ha!" His laugh was pure derision. "Tell me you liked *Raider's Revenge.*"

"I didn't. It was dreadful. I'm amazed Jamison Roswold can direct himself out of bed in the morning. The script wasn't fit to wrap fish in. But I *never* said I hated your portrayal of the Raider."

"Well, you did," Reilly insisted. 'You've never thought I could act worth a damn, and you're probably right. But it irks the hell out of me you get to say so in a hundred and thirteen newspapers every bloody week."

Jayne ignored the second part of his outburst. Her attention zeroed in on the first part. There had been a certain strain in his voice, a certain flash of vulnerability in his eyes. She'd seen it before and hadn't quite been able to interpret it. She concentrated on it now, holding herself very still. Out of habit her fingers of her right hand toyed with the bracelet she never removed from her left wrist. It was silent, but Reilly's expression told her everything she needed to know: Big, tough, cocky Pat Reilly was having a crisis of faith.

He shifted uncomfortably under her steady stare. Jayne felt a surge of sympathy and compassion.

Poor Reilly. If anyone was ill equipped to have an attack of insecurity, it was Pat Reilly. He would see it as a weakness. He would hate himself for it. He would demand more of himself and deliver less, and the circle would spiral down and down.

Unable to stop herself, Jayne reached out and laid a hand on his rigid forearm. The need to reassure him was too strong to resist. She didn't really want to resist it anyway. She liked Reilly. It hurt her to see him hurting.

"I think," she said quietly, earnestly, "that you have a wealth of talent. I think it's a shame that talent has been wasted on second-rate stories. I think it's a shame no director has been astute enough or shrewd enough to help you tap into it. I think you're a very good actor, that with the right project and the right director, you could be great."

Reilly stared down at her warily, wanting to believe her but not quite able to. The conflict built within him until his chest was so tight he could hardly breathe.

"You certainly wowed 'em tonight in that scene you played with me," she said with a touch of irony.

"There wasn't much acting to that," he admitted quietly. "I was too wrapped up in you to concentrate. When I'm with you, I'm no actor at all, Jayne. I'm just a man."

His choice of words made a tiny smile turn her lips. Her heart pounded a little harder as those words sank in. He hadn't been acting. What he gave her was honest emotion. Another of her shields against him fell by the wayside.

Jayne ran her hand up the steel-hard muscles of his arm, frowning prettily. "Look how tense you are. No wonder you can't sleep. Come over here."

Reilly let her lead him along down the steps to the U-shaped sofa. When she ordered him to sit on the floor with his back to the couch, he raised an eyebrow but complied. Jayne settled herself cross-legged onto the soft cushion directly behind him.

"Have you ever had a psychic massage?" she asked. "You tune yourself in to your body and your psychic energy until you achieve harmony with the life energy of the world around you."

"What a lot a crap, Jaynie," he grumbled. "Skip it and get on to the massage part. I could do with some of that."

Jayne made a face at the back of his head. "Take your shirt off."

Reilly shot her a look over his shoulder that was brimming with that old Pat Reilly devilish charm. To her own credit as an actress, Jayne remained impassive. As he peeled the T-shirt off over his head and discarded it, warmth radiated through her midsection. The man had a body that could stop traffic. And she was about to lay her hands on it. Drawing in a long, thin breath, she tried to steady herself, telling herself she was doing this for Reilly's spiritual benefit.

What air her lungs had managed to retain vanished the instant she touched him. His shoulders were like marble, hard and smooth. His tanned skin was warm and vibrant beneath her fingertips. Touching him had nearly the same effect on her as having him touch her. A low groan tried to rise up out of her throat and she just barely managed to suppress it. She did her best to focus her attention on working the knots out of Reilly's muscles and ignoring the knots of sexual tension coiling in her lower body and at the tips of her breasts.

Methodically, her fingers kneaded his shoulders, working down the slope from his neck to his upper arms and back up again. Her thumbs rubbed up and down, gently coaxing the corded muscle to release its tension. Reilly groaned and sighed, unable to hold on to the stress.

"That's it, honey," Jayne murmured softly. "Let all that tension go; you don't need it. Just relax. Doesn't that feel nice?"

"Mmmmmm . . . ," he purred lazily. "I can

only think of a couple of things that would feel nicer. Care to try them?"

Jayne reserved comment and went on with the treatment. "Breathe deep and relax. You have to find your center of being. Stress throws off your cosmic balance."

"Jayne . . ."

His warning tone told her she was going to have to take a different approach. Reilly's beliefs were grounded in things that could be seen and touched. Cosmic life energy was too abstract a concept for him to trust.

"You're a good actor. You're a wonderful actor. I'm sorry you got the impression I thought otherwise. Do you think you're a good actor?"

There was a telling pause before he said, "I do okay."

"You're good," she insisted. "Say it."

"Jayne—"

"Say it, or I'll stop massaging."

"You're bloody cruel, sheila."

"Say it."

"I'm a good actor," he said flatly.

Jayne lifted her hands slightly from his shoulders. "Say it like you mean it."

He heaved a sigh but took her direction. "I'm a good actor."

"You're a very good actor. You've just made lousy decisions about projects. Why did you do *Road Raider*?"

"They offered me a potful of money, and my folks were heavy in debt. They were maybe gonna lose their place. I had a chance to help them out, so I took it. Then *Deadly Weapon* came along. The director was a pal of mine whose last two projects had gone belly-up."

Jayne bit her lip. Her hands slowed, the therapeutic massage drifting into slow caresses. Reilly had made his choices out of a sense of duty. She felt ashamed of herself for ever having thought that he had chosen the pictures he had as an easy way to line his own pockets. She should have known better. He'd never lived extravagantly in Hollywood. Certainly, he'd done his share of partying, but he didn't throw cash around on sports cars or lavish mansions or any of the other customary accoutrements of stardom.

Perhaps she had known better deep down. It had simply been easier to believe the worst of him because that had given her a weapon against the attraction she'd felt for him when she'd been married to Mac. She wondered now what other of her opinions of Reilly were misconceptions, deliberate or otherwise.

"The movies did well enough and nobody seemed willing to offer me anythin' better," Reilly said, confiding in someone for the first time since he couldn't remember when. He'd never even confided in Mac, and Mac had been his best friend. Somehow, just now, with the lights down low and Jaynie rubbing his back, with the fog bank swirling outside and the cozy den full of warmth, it didn't seem all that hard to confide in Jayne. "Besides, I had three brothers and three sisters to put through college, and relatives comin' out of the woodwork, all of them needin' somethin' or other."

Tears rose up in Jayne's eyes. Her heart swelled in her breast until she thought it would burst. What a dear, sweet man he was. She lifted her hand and stroked it over the back of his head, letting the silky strands of his hair sift through her fingers.

"You're a good man, Pat Reilly," she said, leaning toward him, but holding back the urge to wrap her arms around him and hug him.

Reilly turned and looked up at her, his beautiful blue eyes glowing with intensity in the soft light. "Where I come from a man stands by his family and his mates. Bein' good's got nothin' to do with it; that's just the way things are."

"Stubborn man," Jayne complained with a

fond smile. "Didn't your mama ever teach you how to take a compliment?"

"Nope." He turned around and kneeled before the couch, planting a hand on either side of Jayne's hips. He grinned, showing off his famous dimple. "She was too busy chasin' me out of the kitchen, scoldin' me for swipin' her biscuits before they were cool."

She chuckled softly, completely disarmed by his rough charm, completely aroused by the sight of his thickset bare chest. Muscles rippled with his slightest movement. A light furring of tawny hair curled across his pectorals and arrowed down in a line over the washboard muscles of his abdomen, disappearing into the low-riding waist of his sweatpants.

"I suspected as much," she murmured.

"Did you now?" He inched closer.

"Mm-hmm."

He leaned toward her, and it seemed only natural for Jayne to meet him halfway. When his lips captured hers, she didn't allow herself to ask questions, she simply enjoyed. She enjoyed the taste of him, the feel of his whiskers beneath her fingertips as she framed his face with her hands. She enjoyed the subtle textures of his mouth— firmness, silken softness, the velvety rasp of his tongue against hers. It was a gentle kiss, not angry or demanding or possessive. It was wonderful.

A languid dizziness swirled through her head as Reilly kissed her again and again and again, slowly and gently. She felt herself floating and drifting and wasn't entirely sure whether the sensation was a spiritual or a physical one or a combination of both. It abated only slightly when her head and shoulders were lowered to the cushion of the sofa and Reilly settled himself above her.

Some of her doubts about him had been erased. Those remaining were being steadily pushed aside by the passion rising inside her. Jayne made no move to stop it. Nor did she make any move to stop Reilly when his hand slid to the sash of her robe.

He looked down at her, his breath burning his lungs. She was so lovely lying there beneath him. Her dark-fire hair fanned out across the white cushion in a rich contrast of color and texture. Her dark eyes gazed steadily up at him, shining like onyx. She was delicate and feminine, and he'd never wanted anything so badly as he wanted to touch her.

He pulled loose the sash, then ran his hand up the neckline of the robe, touching both the silk of the cloth and the silk of Jayne's exposed skin. His fingertips dipped inside the garment, and he slowly bared her right breast to his ardent gaze. It was small but plump, as dainty and feminine as the rest of her. Even as he admired it, the dusky peach nipple at the center tightened into an inviting little bud.

Not even trying to resist temptation, Reilly lowered his head and brushed his lips across the knotted flesh. Jayne sucked in a breath. A low groan escaped her when he drew his tongue across it and back again. He raised his head a bit and admired the glow of the wetness his mouth had trailed across her breast and the way her nipple tightened and puckered as the air cooled it. Then he lowered his head again and took the distended peak into his mouth and began to suck strongly and rhythmically.

Jayne stirred restlessly. She clutched at Reilly's bare shoulders with her hands and shifted her hips as desire coursed through her, unchecked for the first time in forever. It swept through her like a fire, swirling and leaping, licking at the core of her. Sensations assaulted her one on top of the other—the feel of Reilly's mouth tugging at her nipple, the delicious weight of him bearing down on her, the strength of his arousal pressing into her thigh, the ache of need that throbbed between her own thighs and intensified with each pull of his mouth.

The sensations built and swelled, sweeping her along on a wave that crested abruptly. She gasped, her whole body stiffening and arching up against Reilly's.

"Oh, Jaynie," he whispered reverently.

He watched her face as she reached her peak and then for a long moment as her orgasm gradually subsided. That she had reached it so easily and with so little effort on his part surprised and excited him.

His hand was trembling when he brushed her hair back from her damp forehead. He dropped a kiss on her mouth, then stared down into her eyes, his expression a combination of male pride and sexual hunger.

"I want to be inside you the next time that happens," he said, his voice a graveled purr. "I want to feel you tighten around me. I want you." He leaned closer and feathered hungry kisses down her jaw to her ear, where he nipped her and teased her with his tongue. "Aw, Jaynie, I want you so bad. I've wanted you for so long. Please let me."

Jayne groaned as Reilly kneed her thighs apart and settled himself intimately against her. The thin fabric of his sweatpants was the only barrier between them. There was certainly no question about him wanting her. She wanted him, too. She was tired of forcing herself to deny the unique desire she felt for this man. As she stroked the muscled ridges of his back, her bracelet burned between her flesh and his, and she knew again that sense of inevitability. In what direction this step would take them, she wasn't sure. But this had been their destiny from the first, and there was no point denying it any longer.

"Yes," she whispered.

Reilly raised his head sharply. His gaze could have burned through titanium. "Are you sure, Jaynie? Once it's done, there's no going back. I won't have regrets between us. I won't have any ghosts either. I need you like a dying man needs salvation, but I won't tolerate compromise."

"No," she murmured, relieved that she felt no guilt as she made this decision. "I'm sure."

He stared at her a moment longer, reading every nuance of her expression. Finally he nodded. "All right then."

He levered himself up off her and off the couch, then offered her his hand and helped her up. Jayne's knees swayed unsteadily beneath her, but she managed to lead Reilly the short distance across the den and up the steps to her bedroom.

The room took up the entire east end of the second floor. Three walls were comprised of floor-to-ceiling multipaned windows so that the room seemed to be a platform suspended in the mist. Reilly glanced around with a distracted sense of wonder. His focus was on Jayne, but a part of his brain registered the various aspects of the unique environment she had created for herself.

To the far right, a set of steps led up to a Jacuzzi that was set down in the cedar floor. It was flanked by two walls of glass and surrounded by greenery. In the center of the room stood an over-stuffed love seat, a matching chair, and a low table that had been taken over by an ivy plant. To the far left of the room was the bed. This was what caught Reilly's attention and held it.

Jayne's bed was nothing more than a king-size mattress on a simple pedestal. Rumpled white satin sheets glowed richly in the soft light, seeming like a tangible extension of the mist that swirled outside the window. An assortment of white pillows was scattered across the head like a line of clouds.

She led him now to the side of the big bed and lifted his hand to press a kiss to his calloused palm. Slowly he slid the flowered robe from her shoulders and down the supple line of her back. It dropped with the softest of sighs to pool on the thick white carpet and was forgotten as Reilly feasted his eyes on her.

Jayne was lovely in a sleek, fine way. His gaze drifted down the subtle lines of her, her small proud breasts, her dainty waist, the gentle outward slope of her slim hip. She was so petite, so perfectly feminine, his whole body was trembling at the thought of making her his. His concentration on that thought was so absolute that he jumped when Jayne's hands plucked at the drawstring of his sweatpants.

The pants had done nothing to disguise Reilly's state of arousal. Still, Jayne's breath caught in her throat as she drew the loose fabric slowly down his hips, and a small yearning sound escaped her as she uncovered the proud evidence of his gender. Reilly was impressively male, warm and hard as she closed her hand around him.

He let his head fall back and sucked a breath in through his teeth as he enjoyed the exquisite torture of Jayne's small soft hand stroking him. Desire coiled in his gut until he was sure he couldn't stand any more. As she had done, he lifted her hand and pressed a kiss to her palm then nuzzled the bracelet that hung like a wreath of tiny golden stars around her wrist.

Jayne backed away, her eyes never leaving his,

and settled herself in the center of the bed. The mattress dipped as Reilly joined her. He took her in his arms and stretched out across the cool satin sheets.

As badly as he wanted to prolong the preliminaries, his body was screaming for release. Gently he rolled Jayne beneath him and kneed her thighs apart, reaching between them to test her readiness with a tender caress that wrung a gasp from her. She was warm and moist as he entered her, and so tight he had to ruthlessly check his own response when he was but halfway home. His instincts urged him to bury himself in her with one hard possessive thrust, but he held back, the idea of frightening or hurting her abhorrent to him. The anger and frustration he had aimed at her in the past was gone now. This was the woman he had wanted, had waited for. This, their first time together, had to be perfect.

Jayne let her fingernails sink into Reilly's shoulders as pleasure rippled through her. Sighing his name, she lifted her hips into his, taking all of him. It was magnificent, welcoming him into her body, becoming one with him. He filled her completely, as if this silken pocket of her womanhood had been tailor-made for him. And along with the pleasure that radiated outward from the point of their ultimate union was a sense of rightness, of completion.

Her hands drifted down Reilly's back as he withdrew, cupping his buttocks as he plunged into her again. The muscles beneath her fingers relaxed and tightened as he repeated the process again and again. She arched to meet his thrusts, her heels slipping on the satin sheets as she tried to gain purchase.

"Put your legs around me, luv," Reilly muttered between deep wet kisses.

A groan rumbled deep in his chest as she complied, her smooth limbs wrapping around his hips. He slid a hand between them and caressed her breast, his breath catching hard in his lungs when he rolled her nipple between his thumb and forefinger and her body tightened convulsively around his sex. She was so responsive, so openly giving. She was everything he had dreamed and something extra besides. There was a purity in her lovemaking, no guile, no selfishness, no deception. When she opened her eyes and gazed up at him, he felt enveloped by a power, an energy that transcended anything he'd ever known with a woman.

"That's it, Jaynie," he whispered darkly. "Look

at me. I want to watch your face. I want to see it in your eyes."

In a way, his command was as erotic as anything else going on between them, Jayne thought. He was asking her to share everything with him, not only her physical ecstasy, but the emotional ecstasy that would be mirrored in her eyes as well. In that ultimate moment she would have no secrets from him.

On a deeply instinctive level, that idea frightened Jayne. She would be giving herself to him wholly, body and soul. Reilly, whose passions ran deep and fierce, would own her in the most elemental way. He would consume her, just as she had feared all along. But like a moth drawn to a flame, she couldn't pull away now. Her destiny had been determined, and she gave herself over to it and to him.

She looked up at him as he moved above her and within her, his body reaching inside hers to touch the deepest core of her desire. The muscles of his shoulders and upper arms bunched and flexed as he braced himself over her. The pale white light that flooded the room illuminated the sheen of sweat that slicked his skin. Then her gaze locked on his just as the tension building in her lower body exploded.

Jayne cried out as the shock waves splintered through her. Her climax was so powerful, she actually felt her consciousness dim. She wasn't even certain whether or not she was still looking up at Reilly. His image was indelibly etched in her mind. The neon glow of his blue eyes was something she could feel as well as see. The dark, sexy words he was urgently whispering to her seemed to come to her through a fog as thick as the one outside the windows.

She could feel him imbedded deep within her, throbbing as her body rewarded his efforts with contraction after contraction. Then he wrapped his arms around her, crushing her to his heaving chest. He buried his face against her throat and drove himself into her for three hard strokes. His big body stiffened in her arms, and Jayne gasped again as she felt the warm pulsing of his climax.

Slowly, Reilly rolled to his side and snuggled Jayne against him. He feathered kisses across her face, brushing his lips over her cheeks, her forehead, the tip of her nose, her chin, seemingly intent on branding every inch of her skin with his touch. She hadn't felt so cherished in a long, long time.

Not since Mac.

She was a little surprised that the thought of

the man she had loved so well brought no guilt with it, only a touch of sadness. Mac had been gone from her life for a long time, but now he felt a little farther away.

"No regrets, Jaynie," Reilly murmured.

Jayne glanced up into his eyes, her heart clenching at the worry she saw there. She smiled softly and caressed the rough plane of his cheek. "No. No regrets."

"Mac wouldn't begrudge us being happy together."

"No, he wouldn't." When he started to speak again, she pressed two fingers to his lips to silence him. "No ghosts, Reilly—for either of us."

They were crossing a threshold. Jayne could feel it. She could also feel a knot of apprehension in her stomach, but she did her best to ignore it. It wasn't a premonition, it was plain old fear. She was flying blind into unknown territory with a man she had always considered dangerous. But as Reilly cuddled her to his chest and pressed a kiss on the top of her head, she felt some of her hesitation slide away. She was fast discovering Pat Reilly was a man she could like and respect, a man she could care for, a man she could love.

She just hoped and prayed he could love her in return.

SEVEN

THE KNOCK THAT sounded on the bedroom door was soft, but it woke Jayne immediately. She disentangled herself from Reilly's embrace, sitting up carefully, trying not to wake him. He was sound asleep, his face buried in a pillow, his breathing deep and even. His hair stuck up like a rooster's tail. The sheet rode low across the small of his back. Jayne sighed dreamily and smiled a secret smile. He looked adorable and sexy. It was a huge temptation to lean down and kiss the dip between the muscles of his lower back.

"Jayne?" Candi's voice called out hesitantly. "Are you asleep?"

Jayne jumped guiltily. "Just a second, honey," she whispered loudly.

She eased from the bed and snatched her robe

up from the floor, thrusting her arms into it as she crossed the room and belting it securely before she slipped out the door.

Candi stood with her arms wrapped around her chest, her belly protruding beneath. This girl didn't bear much resemblance to the spike-haired punk she portrayed during the day. This girl was a wide-eyed teenager going through a difficult time in her life. In her long flannel nightgown with no makeup and her hair combed, she looked frightfully young and vulnerable.

"What's the matter, honey?" Jayne asked softly, reaching out to comb a strand of orange-and-black hair from the girl's eyes. "Are you feeling okay?"

Candi shrugged, doing her best to make light of her trip across the house. Heaven forbid anyone should think she needed reassurance or a shoulder to cry on, Jayne thought.

"I couldn't sleep. The baby's moving around a lot and—" She broke off at the sound that rumbled on the other side of Jayne's bedroom door. It sounded decidedly masculine and very much like a snore. Candi's eyes rounded and her mouth dropped open in embarrassment. "Ohmygod. I'm sorry. I interrupted something." She shooed her hands at Jayne as she started leaning back toward the den. "Go back to bed. I'll be fine."

"Don't be silly. You didn't interrupt anything," Jayne said, trying to brazen it out. To her dismay, Reilly chose that moment to begin snoring in earnest. He sounded like a big truck with a bad muffler. Jayne's cheeks turned a shade that matched the fuchsia flowers in her robe.

"It's okay, Jayne," Candi said gently, a smile tugging at her lips.

Jayne pressed her hands to her cheeks and groaned as she dragged them back through her hair. "It's not okay. What kind of example am I setting for you?"

"A pretty terrific one, I think," the girl said honestly. She led Jayne down the steps to the sofa where they settled in side by side. "Do you know what kind of example my folks set? My old man used to come home drunk every night and knock my mother around the house for fun. I don't think either one of them ever knew what it was to love somebody."

Jayne put her arm around the girl's shoulders as Candi's eyes filled with tears and her hand strayed absently to her belly.

"I could hardly believe you were for real when

I moved in here. You care about people. You really want to help."

"I do my best," Jayne murmured self-consciously. A wry smile tugged at her mouth as she remembered Reilly using those same words earlier.

"You're about the only person who ever cared what happened to me."

A lump lodging in her throat, Jayne gave Candi a hug. She was a good kid who'd gotten nothing but bad breaks. It broke Jayne's heart to think of the loveless childhood Candi had survived. "Well, the rest of them missed out, honey, because I think you're a pretty terrific person."

"Thanks," she said with a smile. "I only hope someday somebody can love me the way you love Reilly."

Was it that obvious, Jayne wondered with a start. Lord, she had only just figured it out for herself. Candi had said it as if it were common knowledge. She wondered what Reilly's reaction to the statement would have been. Would he have been as matter-of-fact about it as Candi sounded? Was it common knowledge to him? He had told her he'd come to Anastasia to discover what this thing was that burned between them. What would he do if she told him it was love? He didn't have a very good track record in that area.

"Can you believe Timothy Fieldman asked me to that dance?" Candi asked, trying a little too hard to sound flippant. "What a dork."

"Oh, I don't know," Jayne said, automatically coming to Timothy's defense. "I think it was sweet of him to ask you. You should have accepted."

Candi gave her a look. "Get real. Me at a dance? A costume party, maybe. I could go as the *Hindenburg*."

"It might have been fun."

"Oh, right, with everyone staring at me like I'm some kind of freak. Let's face it, my dancing days are over." Her lower lip settled into a pout that made her look even younger than she was.

Jayne smiled sadly as she realized they were finally getting to the heart of the matter. Candi was feeling left out. At present she seemed to have very little in common with other kids her age. Her pregnancy precluded her from the usual teenage activities. No one was going to ask her to go out for cheerleading or join the swim club. She didn't fit in with anyone's clique.

It made Jayne's heart ache to know Candi was feeling lonely and left out. On the other hand,

Candi had made her own choices. She had since discovered it wasn't fun or glamorous or romantic being sixteen and pregnant. Nor had getting pregnant solved any of her problems; it had instead created a whole set of new ones that were at least as difficult as the old ones. It wasn't going to do any good for Jayne to give her a lecture, though. What Candi needed now was love, support, and guidance.

"It won't be long now, sweetheart," Jayne whispered, coaxing the girl to lay her head on her shoulder. "You've got your whole life ahead of you. So does this little one," she added, pressing a hand to Candi's rounded stomach. The baby on the other side gave her a vigorous kick, and both mother and friend smiled and chuckled.

"Yeah. I hope she gets parents who really love her a lot," Candi said wistfully.

"I'm sure she will, honey."

Reilly watched the two of them, his shoulder braced against the doorway, his arms folded across his bare chest. He had awakened with a jolt, realizing that Jayne was gone from the bed. His first thought had been that she'd gone off to brood about Mac. He was sure she'd been thinking about MacGregor in the aftermath of their lovemaking. He had been too. There was no getting around it—Mac had been a big part of both their lives. But Mac was gone now and Reilly had no intention of taking a backseat to his buddy's ghost.

After pulling on his sweatpants, he had set out to find Jayne and take her back where she belonged—in his arms. It hadn't been an hour since the second time they'd made love, and already his body was aching with hunger for hers. His search had gotten him as far as the doorway.

The scene below sent a soft warmth through him and lodged an unfamiliar knot in his throat. Jayne was curled on the sofa, her arm around her young charge. She spoke to Candi in a voice that was motherly and compassionate. She was quite a woman, his Jaynie. He loved her so much, he thought his heart would burst.

He wondered what she would think if he told her that. It had kind of taken him by surprise. He'd felt something for her ever since the first time they'd met, and he had given it a dozen different names, most of them having something to do with sex. None of the labels had ever quite fit. There had always been some aspect of the feeling that had eluded him when he tried to pin it down in his typically practical manner. Maybe it had been the seed of this love that was now growing within him.

Well, no matter the root of it, he was in love with her now. The question was what to do about it. His own impulsive response was to bind her to him permanently as soon as possible, but he had an idea Jayne would shy away. For all her flakiness, she tended to be cautious with her heart—at least where he was concerned.

He was sure she was in love with him. There had been no mistaking the look in her eyes when he had been poised above her in bed. But she was wary too. Sweeping her off her feet and hustling her to Vegas for a quick ceremony probably wasn't the answer.

They needed some time together. Time for Jayne to grow to trust him. Time for Jayne to see he wasn't a threat, which was essentially what he had been when she'd been married to Mac. Time to see she wasn't going to be just another in a long line of romantic interests. And when she'd had that time, then he'd sweep her off her feet.

He figured it'd take a couple of weeks, a month at the outside.

Pushing himself away from the door, he cleared his throat discreetly so as not to barge in on "woman talk." Both Jayne and Candi looked up at him. Candi wore a smug, knowing smirk. Jayne's cheeks bloomed rosy and her eyes glowed. She looked as if she was feeling a little shy, which surprised him. She sure as hell hadn't been shy with him in bed. The look made him want to scoop her up in his arms and carry her straight back to her room. He refrained out of deference to Candi, and bent to pick up his T-shirt from the arm of the couch instead.

He gave the girl a skeptical look, scratching his chin. "Oh, yeah, I remember you know," he said with a sudden grin. He pulled the black T-shirt over his head and tugged it down. "I didn't recognize you without the spikes."

Candi tossed a pillow at him. "Smart ass."

Reilly turned to Jayne with mock affront. "You gonna let her talk to me that way?"

Jayne snickered. "I always encourage her to tell the truth."

"Women!" he said with a snort. "You can't live with 'em, and you'll never have clean underwear without 'em."

"Why would you care?" Candi asked sarcastically. "It said in *StarBeat* you don't wear any."

"Candi!" Jayne wailed. "For crying out loud!"

Reilly just laughed. "Don't believe everything

you read, little sheila. You're liable to get yourself in trouble."

"Too late for that," Candi quipped, heaving herself up off the sofa. She rubbed her belly and heaved a sigh. "If you two will excuse me, I'm going to go raid the refrigerator. I haven't cheated on my diet yet today."

"How about I make us all a pot of tea?" Jayne offered.

Reilly and Candi groaned in unison. Jayne's tea, made from the herbs she grew on the roof of the dairy parlor, was certifiably horrible. Reilly had sampled it once and likened it to the poison the old aborigines used on their hunting spears.

"Hot chocolate?" Candi asked him.

"Heavy on the chocolate with lots of marshmallows."

"I'll get right on it."

Jayne scowled at both of them, but they ignored her. Candi saluted smartly, turned, and left the room. Her footsteps sounded on the stairs.

"You snore," Jayne said, making her accusation sound like a sin worse than any other.

Reilly's brows lifted in amusement. "Do I?"

"Candi heard you. Snoring. In *my* bedroom!" She huffed an outraged breath, flapping her arms at her sides.

"If you're worried about givin' her ideas, I think she already knows how it's done, luv."

"That isn't the point."

Chuckling, Reilly circled behind Jayne and slid his arms around her, his big hands splaying across her tummy. He bent his head and nibbled at the satin-soft skin beneath her right ear. "Why the blush, Jaynie? I don't recall you blushing when you were kissing my—"

"That was different," Jayne said defensively. "I believe in complete honesty in the physical expression of feelings. The Buddhists teach that sexual honesty between people who care for each other is a key to a plane of higher spiritual enlightenment."

"For once I think I agree with you," he mumbled, nuzzling her cheek. "I also believe two mature adults involved in a caring relationship don't have anything to be ashamed of."

He snuggled her closer, his hands rubbing lazily across the smooth, slightly convex surface of her belly. "Um—this is a bit after the fact, I know, but are we gonna end up like Candi?"

Everything inside Jayne went still at the thought of Reilly's baby growing within her. It stunned her how badly she wanted that. Mac hadn't been able to give her children, and she had accepted that fate. But to have Reilly's baby . . . A fierce longing pierced her heart.

She loved Reilly in the most fundamental way a woman could love a man. The thought frightened her more than a little. She knew her own emotions were strong and true. She didn't fall in and out of love. But what about Reilly—the sexiest man in the universe, the most eligible bachelor in Hollywood, the man whose life energy burned as hot and bright as a comet and who left a trail of broken hearts glowing in his wake?

"Jaynie?"

His voice startled her from her musings. "No. The timing is all wrong."

"Famous last words," he said with a wry chuckle. Deftly, he turned her in his arms and dropped a kiss on the tip of her little nose. "Not that I'm against the idea, mind you. I kinda like the thought of fillin' this big barn up with little Reillys."

Jayne blushed, more with pleasure at the thought and with his admission than with embarrassment. "Is that a fact?"

"Mmm . . . that would keep you out of mischief—chasing the little nippers around, changing nappies all day. Think of all the innocent movies that would be saved from that razor tongue of yours."

She gave him a narrow-eyed look. "Berg's Drugstore is on the corner of Fourth and Kilmer."

Reilly's face dropped into a scowl as Jayne backed out of his arms and moved toward the hall. He planted his suddenly empty hands on his hips. "You mean you want me to—"

"That's right, Big Daddy," Jayne said with a feline smile.

Reilly sputtered, his face turning red. "I can't go into a corner drugstore and buy—Bloody hell, it'd be in every paper from here to Sydney!"

"Wear your disguise, Romeo," Jayne suggested, giggling at his obvious and very uncharacteristic embarrassment. "I can't believe you haven't bought more than your fair share of prophylactics over the years, Reilly. What do you usually do—buy them mail order by the gross?"

He caught the faint but distinct ring of jealousy in her voice. While it pleased him, he wasn't going to have it be an issue between them. In three strides he cut off her escape route. She tried to dodge away from him, but he caught her with embarrassing ease and pulled her close.

"Let's get this right straightaway, luv. I've

known my share of ladies, I don't deny it, but I don't carve notches in my bedposts."

Jayne frowned. "They're probably brass."

"You don't believe all those gossip rag rumors about me, do you?"

"If I believed only half of them, I'd know better than to get involved with you."

He ignored her remark. His attention was focused on the delectable curve of her throat as she arched her head back to look at him. He traced the line of it with his thumb.

"You're the only woman I've had on my mind or anywhere else for a long time, Jaynie," he murmured. "You've got my word on that."

And Pat Reilly was nothing if not a man of his word, Jayne thought, rising up on tiptoes to meet his kiss.

Maybe there was a chance that their romance would work out after all. Maybe he was going to prove to be the exception to the rule of fickle actors. The way he made her feel when he kissed her left Jayne thinking she had no other choice but to find out. Reilly may have unsettled her and overwhelmed her and knocked her off her cosmic center of oneness with the universe, but he was one heck of a kisser, and she loved him like she never thought she'd love another man again.

"Stand very still," Bryan instructed.

"What are you going to do?" Alaina asked. Motionless, she wore a look of wary concentration and a Ralph Lauren ensemble. On her head was perched a shiny black top hat. They were standing in the small yard next to the converted dairy parlor, a benevolent sun shining down on them, cutting the chill of the breeze that came inland off the ocean. "There isn't going to be a live animal on my head when you take this thing off, is there?"

Bryan made no answer but looped his arms around her neck and slowly drew them back, flipping the hat off with a flourish. Alaina remained still, but her cool blue eyes narrowed at the frown on Bryan's face.

"What? Bryan, I love you like a brother, but if there's an animal on my head, I'll pound you."

He lifted down a scrawny gray kitten and petted it absently. It looked up at him and mewed.

"I don't understand what went wrong," he said morosely. "It was supposed to be a bouquet of silk flowers."

While he dug a scrap of paper out of his shirt pocket and jotted himself a note, Alaina brushed frantically at her fifty-dollar hairstyle and swore a blue streak.

"You know I want to help," she said, shaking a finger at him. "You've always been there when I needed you, and I want to be here for you. But you promised you wouldn't put animals on me!"

Bryan pushed his glasses up on his nose and looked hurt. "I didn't mean to put an animal on your head. I don't understand what's going wrong. I used to be able to do that trick with my eyes closed. I've completely lost my magic!" he said, throwing his hands up in the air, apparently forgetting he held a cat in one of them.

Alaina snatched the kitten away from imminent danger and set it down on the ground where it wasted no time scampering away. She took Bryan's big hand in hers and kissed his knuckles. "It hasn't been that long since you lost Serena, Bryan. Give yourself some time. What you need is a distraction." She stood back and turned to the side. "What do you think? Do you think I look fat? I'm not big enough for maternity clothes yet, but I think I look fat."

A lopsided smile tugged at Bryan's mouth. "I think you look fabulous. You're glowing."

"I'd better be glowing," she said dryly. "Forty-five bucks for face cream. If I'm not glowing, I'm going back to Sak's and cram that bubblehead of a clerk into the jar."

"And they say mothers-to-be are serene," Jayne commented as she rounded the corner of the milk parlor.

"I love being pregnant," Alaina insisted. "It's the sensory deprivation that's getting on my nerves. I haven't had a cigarette in twelve weeks, three days, and seventeen hours."

Jayne gave her friend a consolatory pat on the shoulder and changed the subject. "Have either of you seen Reilly?"

"I saw him heading down to the llama barn," Bryan said. He gave Jayne a long look. "Are you trying to find him or avoid him?"

"Find him." She looked from friend to friend, hoping to find some kind of reassurance that giving her heart to Reilly was the right thing to do. "What do you think?"

Bryan didn't need to answer aloud. Jayne knew immediately he had no answers for her. He had all he could do to get himself from one day to the next. His ability to sense the feelings of others had deserted him as he focused on his own shattered emotions. He simply shrugged and looked apologetic.

"He seems like a good guy," he said. "What does your bracelet tell you?"

"Nothing." She lifted her arm and tapped a finger against the key as if she thought she could somehow jar it into working. She turned a worried look toward Bryan. "Do you think it's a bad omen?"

Alaina made a face. "I'd think it would be worse if you said it did talk to you. Chatting with jewelry is just cause to have a person declared loony. Not that there's ever been a question here," she teased dryly, her eyes twinkling.

Bryan smiled reassuringly and tapped the tip of her nose with his pencil. "Keep the faith, sweetheart. You and Reilly will work things out."

"I think he's gorgeous," Alaina commented, sitting down on a stump. She pulled off a Gucci loafer and rubbed at her swollen foot. "He's one of my favorite actors. I can't wait for *Deadly Intent* to come out."

Jayne jumped as if she'd been stuck with a needle. Her heart lurched into overdrive. "What?"

"*Deadly Intent*. You know, the sequel to *Deadly Weapon* and *Deadly Encounter*. It's supposed to come out this summer, isn't it?"

"I'd forgotten," she murmured, a chill running through her.

It wasn't significant, she told herself as she left her friends and headed for the llama barn. So *Deadly Intent* was about to be released. So what? Reilly hadn't once mentioned it to her. He probably just assumed she knew it was coming out and that she was going to dislike it as much as she had disliked its predecessors, so he hadn't brought the subject up.

Chances were she *would* dislike it. The thought made her feel uncomfortable. In view of Reilly's current state of insecurity concerning his talent, he didn't need bad reviews. What would happen if she had to give him one? Her stomach churned at memories of fickle actors and fragile egos.

It was a situation they were going to have to face eventually. Reilly didn't like what she did for a living. Her profession inevitably clashed with his. They were going to have to deal with that problem as they would have to deal with their other differences.

But not today, Jayne decided as she caught sight of him in the pasture beyond the barn. Today she wanted to concentrate on the present, on the bond that had been strengthening between her and Reilly over the past week of lovemaking. Their relationship seemed to be finding footing on firmer ground as they spent time together, discovering each other, developing their friendship.

She smiled now as she watched him standing a short distance from her llamas. He looked big and tough and handsome in his faded jeans and an old red sweatshirt. The sea breeze ruffled his golden hair, and he squinted against the brilliance of the late afternoon sun.

She was learning so much about him so quickly. She knew he preferred beer to champagne and that he ate enough fried eggs and red meat to make a dietician cringe. He valued his family and his friends, but he felt pressured by them because of his sound financial situation and their constant lack of money. He missed Australia but not vegemite. He swore like a sailor but always said grace at the dinner table.

He hadn't offered all that information; it wasn't in Reilly to talk about himself, which was probably why he rarely gave interviews. These were traits Jayne had observed. As a critic, she was trained to watch closely and carefully, to read body language and the subtle nuances of expression and speech. In truth, she had honed these abilities at an early age. Growing up on the wrong side of the paddock at one of Kentucky's premier thoroughbred farms had given her the unique opportunity to observe a completely different lifestyle from her own. She had spent much of her youth watching the goings-on at the big house from afar, taking in all the details of the lives of her father's wealthy employers.

Now, as she let herself out of the barn and made a beeline across the pasture, she let her powers of observation take in the scene before her. Reilly stood with his hands on his hips and a grin tugging at his mouth. Rowdy stood in front of him, eyes glued on the group of llamas grazing placidly beneath a wind-twisted cypress tree. The sheepdog appeared totally engrossed in the animals even though the llamas didn't seem the least bit interested in Rowdy.

"He thinks they're mutant sheep," Reilly said with a chuckle. "He can't figure out why they won't pay any attention to him."

"Is he an honest-to-goodness sheepdog?" Jayne asked.

"Is he? I'll have you know, Rowdy's won more than his share of competitions. He was one of the best headin' dogs in Willoughby."

He called the dog's name sharply and gave a series of commands, whistling signals that put the dog through his paces. Jayne watched with delight as Rowdy followed his master's orders and tried to herd her uncooperative llamas, dashing around them, creeping toward them as he tried to mesmerize them with his eyes.

Mascara ignored him totally. Pinafore and Petticoat trotted around in circles, their big brown eyes wide with surprise. Jodhpur, the ringleader of the group, quickly became annoyed with the game. He faced off with Rowdy, lowering his head and pinning his long ears back.

"Uh-oh," Jayne said, nibbling at her thumbnail. "You'd better call Rowdy back. He's about to get—Uck! Slimed!"

The llama spit, hitting the sheepdog square in the face with a gob of bilious green goo. Rowdy howled, wheeled, and headed back to his master with his short tail between his legs. Jodhpur raised his long neck and pranced around the fringe of his peer group, immensely proud of himself. The female llamas hummed at him as if in praise of his gallant efforts to defend them from the canine menace.

Reilly doubled over laughing. Jayne tried to contain her chuckling so as not to make Rowdy feel bad. After rolling in the grass to dislodge the gunk, the dog dropped to the ground at his master's feet, planted his head on his paws, and looked woebegone.

"Poor old guy," Reilly said, sinking to his knees in the lush grass. He scratched behind the dog's ears. "Done in by an overgrown goat. Good thing your mates weren't here to see it."

Jayne went to her pets to reassure them and to scratch their long necks as each vied for her attention. Reilly joined her momentarily. Rowdy slinked away in disgrace.

"Why llamas?"

"Because llamas are wonderful."

As if that explained everything. Reilly gave her a look and leaned back skeptically as Jodhpur reached toward him with a curious light in his eye. "They smell like wet rugs and spit in your face. I don't see anything too bloody wonderful about that."

"Hush," Jayne scolded. "Llamas are very sensitive. They'll know it if you don't like them."

"Yeah, well, I think they're weird," he said, taking another step back just in case. "What good are they?"

"They're loyal and sweet," she said, stroking her pets who were viewing Reilly with cool looks. "They have very nice wool—"

"Which you never harvest," he speculated smugly.

Jayne narrowed her eyes at him, knowing he

enjoyed teasing her. There was always going to be some of the boy in Reilly, ever eager to tug a girl's braids. "I'll have you know that llamas are wonderful pack animals."

He lifted a brow. "These llamas?"

She dodged his gaze and committed a minor sin of omission. "I have a full compliment of packs and camping gear for them."

"Is that a fact?"

She crossed her arms over her chest and nodded. "It is."

"Well, I guess they're nicer than tarantulas," Reilly said, chuckling as he worked one of her hands free and tugged her away from her strange pets. She trailed reluctantly after him, pretending to have her nose out of joint.

"Is it time to leave for rehearsal already?" he asked.

"No."

"Just couldn't stay away from me, eh?" he teased, tweaking her nose.

Jayne batted his hand away but couldn't quite keep from grinning. She plopped down on the ground beside him and arranged her full skirt around her. It was unnerving the way he made her feel like a teenager with her first boyfriend. The feeling was alternately marvelous and terrifying.

It was so very different from what she'd felt with Mac. With Mac she had felt peaceful and safe. He had been the bedrock of her existence. Reilly was more like an earthquake, rattling her to her spiritual foundation. She couldn't stay away from him, and she still couldn't decide if that was ultimately good or bad.

Reilly looked at Jayne and shook his head in wonder. She wore an old navy-blue Notre Dame sweatshirt, yet another of her wildly flowered skirts, and a wide-brimmed straw hat tied down with a long white silk scarf. She looked absurd, but absolutely beautiful. He couldn't begin to explain it.

Impulsively, he reached over and tugged the scarf loose so that her hat fell off, spilling her wild mane around her shoulders in glorious disarray.

"So what brings you to the outlands, Calamity Jayne?"

"Bad news, I'm afraid," she said, making an apologetic face. "Remember how you wanted your presence in Anastasia to remain essentially a secret? Well, I just got a call from a stringer for one of the tabloids asking if I knew anything about your getting involved in a play up here. I told him no, but you know how they are. . . ."

Reilly scowled. He certainly did know how

they were. They were parasites, piranha, putrid abscesses feasting on the flesh of celebrities. His broad shoulders rose and fell on a long sigh. He didn't relish the thought of being hounded by reporters and the fans that would follow them. These last few days of relative anonymity had been wonderful. He had been able to relax and let his guard down. He'd been able to concentrate on Jayne rather than the pressures of his career.

Jayne leaned over and kissed his cheek. "I'm sorry."

"It was bound to happen, luv. I guess I'm surprised it didn't happen sooner. It's not your fault." He flashed her a sudden brilliant grin, his dimple winking at her as he leaned close. "I wouldn't object to your tryin' to console me, though."

"Oh, no," Jayne said, leaning back. "I don't want you smiling at me like that, Pat Reilly."

He turned up the wattage on his famous grin yet another notch. "Why's that?"

"Because," Jayne said, trying to catch a decent breath, "when you smile at me like that, it gets me right here." She pressed a hand to her tummy and shuddered. "And I get all flustered and it goes to my head and I can't think straight."

Reilly leaned a little closer, his brilliant blue

eyes dancing with teasing lights. "Here I thought that was your natural state."

Jayne gave him a look, but swallowed hard as her gaze was caught in the tractor-beam of his magnetism. He reached over and covered the hand she'd pressed to her stomach with one of his own.

"You feel it right here?" he asked, his voice as seductive as black satin sheets. Slowly he slid both his hand and hers upward to cup her breast. "Are you sure you don't feel it here?"

Her only answer was a weak moan. Beneath her own palm she could feel her nipple harden with excitement. Erotic sensations zipped through her at the speed of light. Reilly manipulated her hand with his, squeezing the soft globe of her breast, rubbing across the tightening bud of her nipple, all the while watching Jayne's face intently. Her eyelids grew heavy. She wet her lips as she tried to gulp in a breath of air.

Leaning over her, Reilly lowered her to the lush carpet of grass and stretched out beside her, propping himself up on his free arm.

"Do you like that, luv?" he asked in his dark voice. Slowly he drew her hand down across her belly to the apex of her thighs and exerted a gentle pressure there, wringing another moan from her. "Or do you like this better?"

"Reilly," Jayne managed, "don't. Not here."

"Why not?" he asked, lazily massaging her with her own hand.

"We're right out in the open. Anyone could come along and see us."

"That's half the fun, sweet. Doesn't it excite you to think someone could catch us at a crucial moment?"

It did, but Jayne couldn't quite bring herself to admit it. Credo of sexual honesty or not, she'd still been raised a Baptist. "You're wicked."

"Uh-huh," he admitted readily.

His hand found its way under her voluminous skirt and swept up her silken thigh. Regardless of her protests she opened her legs for him ever so slightly as he slipped two fingers inside the leg of her panties and began to explore her most sensitive flesh.

Jayne gasped and made an effort to squirm away from him. "Reilly, not here," she begged. "The llamas are watching."

He looked over to find that the shaggy creatures were indeed watching. It was a little disquieting but not enough to thwart his hormones. He wanted Jayne, and his appetite for her was strong and immediate.

"They're just llamas, Jaynie. What do they care?"

"Well . . . what if they're not just llamas? What if they're beings in their third or fourth incarnation? That could be my Grandma Bessie watching us!"

Reilly's hand stilled. He looked down at her in utter disbelief. "What?! Where do you get this malarkey?"

"It's not malarkey," she protested. Sitting up she pushed his hand out from under her skirt and primly tucked her legs beneath her. "Many of the great religions were founded on the principles of reincarnation," she said, her dark eyes solemn. "I haven't quite decided if I believe in it or not. I'm sort of leaning toward the pool of life energy theory. But, just in case . . ."

She was serious. Reilly sat up, propping his elbow on his knee and plucking his chin in his hand. He watched Jayne tie her hat back on, torn between anger, frustration, and laughing out loud. He chose the latter, laughing wearily as he rubbed a hand across his face. She was so sweet and so earnest in all her goofy convictions, he couldn't bring himself to be angry with her. His body was throbbing with frustrated need, but

Jayne would ease that later, when they were in the privacy of her room.

He pushed himself to his feet and offered her a hand up.

"Aw, Jaynie, you're one of a kind. I love you," he said simply, as casually as if he'd said it every day of his life.

Jayne stopped dead and stared at him as he started to walk away toward the barn. He loved her. Just like that. No hoopla, no ceremony. He just loved her. No big deal.

Questions and anxieties buzzed around in her head like a swarm of angry bees. Was it a big deal, or did Reilly casually toss off declarations of love to whomever? Love wasn't something she took lightly, but Reilly didn't seem flustered in the least.

He shot her a glance over his shoulder. "Come on, sheila. Shake a leg or we'll be late for rehearsal."

EIGHT

JAYNE HAD NEVER lived through anything quite like the two weeks following the press's discovery of Reilly's whereabouts. After the initial call from the tabloid reporter, the leak in their security quickly cracked wide open. In short order Anastasia was overflowing with reporters and fans, all eager for a glimpse—or a piece—of Pat Reilly.

It was a case of mass hysteria unlike anything Jayne had ever imagined. They followed him everywhere. Mobs of them. It had become necessary to post guards at the theater doors. Reilly had reserved rooms in every motel, hotel, and inn in the area to keep everyone guessing as to where he was actually staying.

"Something like this happened on *Star Trek* once," Jayne said as she and Reilly met on a deserted side street three blocks down from the theater. Even from there they could see the swarms lying in wait at the building's main entrance. "Captain Kirk and the whole landing party went onto this planet where once a year the whole population just went nuts and ran around the streets screaming and carrying on." She frowned at the similarities. "I never thought that would happen here. Isn't life strange?"

Reilly preferred a stronger word for it, preceded by a string of colorful adjectives. He'd damn near had it with being the centerpiece of a three-ring circus. He hadn't anticipated the interest his absence from L.A. would spark. Everyone in the business or clinging to the fringes of it wanted to know why he was in Anastasia doing community theater for el zippo money when he could have been stuffing his pockets with his advance for *Road Raider Part III*. On top of that was the interest that blasted article in *WE* had generated. He was going to strangle his publicist for arranging that. Not once in his thirty-two years had he yearned to be known as the sexiest man in the universe.

And the worst part of all this hoopla was the way it was interfering with his courtship of Jayne. Things had been progressing so well until the press had descended on them. Suddenly they were living in a fish bowl, and Jayne hadn't taken to it at all. She had pulled back, retreated to her role as observer rather than participant, watching the mayhem swirl around him, but not allowing it to touch her.

She had not pulled away from him physically. They had managed to outwit the hordes so far; no one had yet discovered where Reilly was staying. They managed to escape the madness for a few hours every night after returning to Jayne's house via an elaborate escape route. And every night she willingly came into his arms. But emotionally she had begun to distance herself. He could sense the hesitancy in her. She was having second thoughts about being involved with him, and Reilly didn't like it one bit. His patience, which was limited at best, was frayed right down to the nub.

"It's creepy the way people follow you around," Jayne grumbled, giving voice to some of her own impatience. It unnerved her the way fans—particularly female fans—sought Reilly out. They were willing to do literally anything to get his attention. Hotel keys and frilly bits of lingerie had been left at the stage door for him every night, along with sacks full of fan mail, written marriage proposals, and proposals that weren't anywhere near as honorable.

It was intimidating in the extreme. For a few days Jayne had allowed herself to believe she could have Reilly all to herself, and that had been wonderful—to pretend she could be the center of his universe and he could be hers. But that was not the case. She was going to have to share him with an overly adoring, mostly female public. If she was going to have a relationship with him, she was going to be swept up into the madness that surrounded him. The sense of peace and sense of place she had worked so hard to attain would be blown right out of the water.

And where would she be left if one of the many lovely ladies ready to throw themselves at Reilly's feet, or any other part of his delectable male anatomy, snagged the actor's attention? Jayne loved him, but she would never bathe him in the kind of blind adoration some would, the kind actors of her acquaintance had demanded from their partners—one after another after another.

"I didn't invite them here," Reilly snapped.

"I didn't say you did," Jayne snapped back.

Stewing, they stalked off down the deserted side street. They took the secret route to the theater, creeping through a series of alleys and buildings that adjoined the theater building. Jayne carried a gigantic ring of keys which she sorted

through as they went. She let them into the hardware store, where they had to go down into the
basement to get into Liebowitz Deli, where they
had to go through a meat locker to get to Bab-
bette's Hypnosis and Tanning Parlor. The last leg
of their incredible journey was to climb out a second-story window at Marx Appliance Barn and
scramble down the fire escape then dash across
the alley to the side door of the theater.

"I hope you appreciate what I'm going through
for you," Jayne said as she made her way down
the fire escape. "I moved here to find spiritual
tranquility. I don't think anybody ever found spiritual tranquility on a fire escape."

Above her, Reilly ground his teeth. Spiritual
tranquility? He had a different name for the reason Jayne had moved to Anastasia—cowardice.
But he bit his tongue on that word.

"Oh, pardon me," he said, unable to keep all
his frustration at bay. "Whose stupid play is it I'm
donatin' my time to?"

Jayne dropped the last three feet to the wet
pavement and brushed a wild snarl of mist-damp
hair out of her eyes. She glared at Reilly as he
joined her, looking rugged instead of rumpled. "If
you think it's stupid, then why are you here when

you could be throwing your career away on some sorry excuse for a movie instead?"

"I'm here because I made a promise."

So they were back to that, were they? He'd made a promise and his code of honor demanded he keep it. It wasn't the line she'd wanted to hear and her expression clearly said so. Beyond that one careless declaration of love delivered two weeks before, Reilly had made no mention of his feelings, and Jayne had been too afraid of getting the wrong answer to ask. She wanted him here because he loved her, not out of some sense of obligation.

Hurt, she stared up at him and willed her chin to stop trembling. "If that's your only reason, then you can leave," she said. "You've kept your promise."

"Aw, Jaynie," Reilly said on a long sigh. His breath silvered the damp night air. He slid his arms around her and drew her unyielding form into his embrace. It was like holding a post. "Don't let's fight, okay?" The leather of his jacket squeaked as he rubbed Jayne's back through the army surplus coat she wore over her dress. "I know the press and the rest are a pain in the neck. They'll lose interest in a day or two."

"You said that two weeks ago."

"Maybe they'll stay for the performance," he said, changing tracks. "Think of the money that'll mean for your young artists. That's what you want, isn't it?"

Jayne nuzzled her cheek against the warmth of his flannel shirt, breathing in the scents that always made her think of Reilly—leather, soap, and man. She felt unaccountably miserable. "I don't know what I want," she mumbled, secretly cursing her bracelet for not providing her with an answer to that question.

"Do you want me?" Reilly questioned in a sexy voice, his hands drifting down to bracket her hips and lift her against him. It was a query with more than one meaning, and he wanted a yes on both counts, but now was not the time to push Jayne. Even he could see that.

Jayne dodged the playful kisses he tried to plant on her mouth and cheeks. She couldn't help but chuckle. "We're in an alley," she pointed out.

"Yeah," he murmured against her throat. "Ever done it in an alley?"

"No and I'm not going to start now," she said primly, even though a panorama of steamy alley scenes was playing through her fertile imagination.

Reilly set her down and shrugged as they moved through the shadows toward the theater door. "Don't know what you're missing, luv," he said cockily.

With a wry smile, Jayne shook her head and sorted through her jumble of keys. There was one thing she could always count on: Reilly's libido.

"There he is!" The cry went up followed by a volley of screams and the thunder of feet on pavement as a crowd stampeded toward them down the alley. "It's Reilly! It's Pat Reilly!"

There was another thing she could always count on, Jayne reflected with a sinking heart: Reilly's fans.

They made it into the building in the nick of time, slamming and bolting the door behind them. The rest of the cast and crew stared at them with looks of mingled amazement and worry. They looked like the occupants of the Alamo, maintaining their vigil while an overwhelming army swarmed outside the gates.

Jayne forced a bright smile. She was, after all, their spiritual leader. She was the one who wanted to encourage people to join the theater and get involved. "Isn't this fun?"

Marlene Desidarian shook a meaty finger at her, a dozen copper bracelets rattling on her wrist. "I told you you had your work cut out." She pointed accusingly at Reilly. "His aura glows red."

"I could have foretold all of this by reading his palm," Wanda Styles said in a husky voice. She patted her hand against her chest, which was mostly exposed by the low-cut black dress she wore. Her inch-long red nails glowed under the stage lights. Tonight she had a spider ring on each finger.

Reilly inched behind Jayne for protection. Wanda Styles was the closest thing to a witch he ever cared to encounter. Not that he was superstitious or anything. He was just none too keen on the idea of Wanda reading his palm or any other part of him.

"I can't imagine how all those people found out Mr. Reilly was here," Cybill Huntley mused. "I only told my mother . . . and my husband . . . and my hairdresser."

"I only told my secretary," Phil Potts said. "And she only told her card club."

So much for swearing people to secrecy, Jayne thought as she looked at her guilty cast. No matter. This had probably all been predestined anyway. It was a test, Jayne thought morosely, wondering whether she and Reilly would pass or fail.

Arnie Von Bluecher stepped forward, looking earnest and enormous. "You vant I should go out and chase dem away from de door, Jayne?"

"No thanks, Arnie. I think Deputy Skreawupp is out there. He can handle things."

On the other side of the door a voice boomed.

"Break it up you people. Show's over. Go on home, or I'll bust you all like ripe melons, and I can do it."

Jayne sighed and turned her attention to work. "Okay, everybody, let's get to it. We have just one more week of rehearsal. I want to polish up Act Three tonight, then we'll take the weekend off because, Lord knows, we could all use a break."

Reilly sat alone in the wings during the first two scenes, watching Jayne work. She was good. Too good to be wasting her time reviewing other people's work. Her directing instincts were very strong, and she had a knack for getting the most out of her actors. The cast of *A Taste of Starlight* were rank amateurs, yet Jayne had them relaxed and into their characters, so involved in what they were doing, they would likely forget there was an audience watching them come performance time. Even Cybill, who had been too nervous to speak at the first rehearsal, was hamming it up in her role as the nightclub singer. Jayne had managed to convey to her people that acting was more than simply reading lines and taking direction, it was becoming a whole other person with a certain way of speaking and moving and thinking.

She had an uncanny eye for detail, for expression and vocal inflection and timing. With nothing more than a suggestion for a head movement or a pause in the middle of a sentence, she could make a scene come alive.

Reilly wondered how she would do behind a camera. His own gut instincts told him she would be good. Heaven knew, she'd gotten more out of him in the few weeks they'd spent on this little play than most of the film directors he'd worked with during his career. She had him working through the wall of insecurity that had sprung up so suddenly in his path. She had him moving forward instead of bolting around side to side like a frightened horse. She had him focusing on positive thoughts rather than negative fears. And those massages she kept giving him weren't hurting anything either.

Reilly knew he had come to Anastasia in part to escape his insecurity. Instead, Jayne had helped him get on the road to defeating it. She had bolstered his confidence in himself.

He owed her a lot, his little Jaynie, and he meant to pay her back. Pat Reilly wasn't a man to let a good turn go unrewarded.

Making certain Jayne was still absorbed in helping Marlene and Wanda through their big fight scene with Phil, he picked up his script and pulled another script from inside it—*Everlasting* by Jayne Jordan.

• • •

"You'll be a star, Desiree," Reilly said, gazing lovingly into the eyes of his leading lady. He pushed his prop glasses up on his nose with his middle finger—exactly the way Bryan did it.

Jayne giggled to herself. Reilly, who had become fast friends with Bryan, had adopted many of Bryan's mannerisms and expressions to use in his role as Wilson Mycroft. They fit wonderfully. Wilson was serious and studious and true-hearted, like Bryan. He seemed to be forever helping friends out of tough spots, like Bryan. Always rooting for the underdog and pushing his glasses up on his nose. And he made a wonderful foil for the saucy, sassy Desiree.

"And you'll never have to wear another chicken suit again," Cybill said. She looked out where the audience would be sitting and smiled. "Is that a happy ending, or what?"

Jayne rose from her seat in the third row and clapped exuberantly. "Very good! I think we should wait about two beats after that last line for the applause, and then close the curtain on a kiss. The crowd would love it," she said, nearly choking on her own suggestion. She didn't much like the idea of Reilly kissing someone else, but this was for the sake of art, after all.

As if he had read her mind, Reilly winked at her. Jayne felt warmed from the inside out. Out of habit, she hooked two fingers through her bracelet, but she refused to wonder why it wasn't giving her any feelings. Maybe she had a feeling overload or a temporary feeling block, or the powers had somehow worn off or something, she rationalized. She told herself she wasn't worried about it . . . not much anyway.

She had plenty of other things to worry about. Getting home in one piece, for instance.

"Who wants to run interference?" she asked as the group prepared to disband for the weekend.

"Arnie and I will take the front door," Marlene volunteered. As the two moved shoulder to shoulder toward the main entrance, the only way to tell them apart was by Marlene's long silver-blond braid swaying across her broad back.

"Come on, Timothy." Candi tugged on young Fieldman's shirt sleeve. "We'll go out the back and occupy the tabloid reporters. We can tell them I'm having Bigfoot's baby."

"Oh, gosh, Candi." Timothy gulped nervously, his Adam's apple bounding up and down in his throat. "I don't know. I didn't much like it that night you told them I'd been abducted and held prisoner by space aliens who performed bizarre sexual experiments on me."

Candi scowled at him. "What are you complaining about? You made the cover of the *Weekly Globe Report*, didn't you?"

Chuckling, Reilly helped Jayne with her coat and pulled her into his arms for a quick kiss. "I think Candi is enjoyin' all this."

"And you're not?" Jayne asked with false surprise.

"I'll tell you what I'd enjoy," he murmured, rubbing his nose against hers. "I'd enjoy havin' you all to myself for the weekend."

"I'd like that, too." Jayne sighed.

There might have been a thread of desperation in her voice. She wouldn't have denied it. She was feeling nervous. The world and all its craziness was closing in on her. She longed to recapture some of the peace she'd had just a month before and share it with the man she loved. She longed to have some kind of reassurance from Reilly that what they had begun to build had a chance to survive over the long haul.

Reilly studied the vulnerable lights in Jayne's jet eyes. He knew how she was feeling—wary, uncertain of this fragile love that was in danger of being trampled by his notoriety. His biggest fear was that she would stand back and watch it happen rather than plunge in and try to take charge of the situation, that she would play the critic rather than the director.

"Well, I dare you to make it happen," he challenged, a truculent gleam in his eyes. He set his chin at an angle that emphasized the sexy cleft in it.

"What? How?" Jayne sputtered.

"You're the director," he said with an arrogant lift of his broad shoulders. "Direct us an uninterrupted weekend."

"This ain't quite what I had in mind, Jaynie," Reilly said through his teeth as they claimed a small corner table.

The bar was crowded shoulder to massive shoulder with fishermen and loggers and their ladies out for a rip-roaring Friday night. The smoke that hung in the air was no thinner than the fog that had descended outside. Loud conversation and the clink of glasses nearly drowned out the Judds wailing from the jukebox.

Jayne's eyes twinkled with mischief. "What's the matter? Don't you like the disguise I picked for you, Aunt Patty?"

Reilly grumbled and snarled as he plunked his big pink handbag down on the table top. "Your aunt Patty," he said on a growl, everything about his tone and his demeanor suggesting utter disgust.

Jayne had cheerfully raided the prop and costume room backstage at the theater. In short order Pat Reilly had been transformed. He was not, however, pleased with the results.

"I think it's the perfect outfit." Jayne beamed with pride. "You look very striking in periwinkle; it brings out your eyes."

"My eyes," he snarled, hooking a big blunt-tipped finger inside the high lace-trimmed collar that was nearly strangling him.

"It's the perfect ruse," Jayne said, leaning close so only Reilly could hear her. "Hiding in plain sight. The Indians used to do it all the time. Of course, they relied more heavily on a psychic wall, you know, a metaphysical defense shield. You could try that. Concentrate on making yourself invisible—"

"Jayne . . ."

She smiled innocently and dropped the mystical talk without missing a beat. "No one would expect you to be sitting in Dylan's Bar dressed as an old lady."

Reilly scowled at her. He supposed he'd asked for this, but it was bloody humiliating. If anyone did recognize him, he'd never live it down. He could just imagine the ribbing he'd get back home if his mates ever found out he'd gone into a bar wearing a dress and pink pumps.

"Candi did a wonderful job with the makeup and wig," Jayne said, reaching out to pat the silver curls coiffed around Reilly's less-than-feminine features. He may have been one heck of a handsome man, but he made one ugly woman, she thought, biting back a grimace. "I can hardly even make out your five-o-clock shadow."

Reilly refused to comment. His attention had drifted to the low-scoop neckline of Jayne's dress. When she leaned across the table, it gaped away just enough to give him a glimpse of the tops of her breasts.

"Reilly . . . ," she said between her teeth. She sat back and discreetly tugged up her bodice. "For Pete's sake! My aunt Patty never looked at me like that!"

His eyes glowed with a sensual heat designed to ignite fires in a woman. "You can bet she never thought what I'm thinkin,' either."

"Oh, I don't know," Jayne said, suddenly contemplative. She tore her gaze away from Reilly's and fanned herself with a cocktail napkin. It would probably give their game away if she leaped across the table and attacked him. She turned her thoughts toward her family back in Kentucky and away from the seductive messages Reilly's male aura was sending her way. "Uncle Duke always had a smile on his face."

"Good evening, Jayne," Dylan Harrison said in cordial welcome as he set down a basket of pretzels. "Who's your lady frie—"

He broke off in midword, his expression going through a comical metamorphosis. Friendliness gave way to shock, which gave way to a kind of stunned confusion.

"It's Reilly," Jayne whispered to Alaina's husband. The look Reilly gave her could have melted stone. She ignored him and said loudly to Dylan, "Dylan, meet my aunt Patty."

Dylan pressed his lips together in an effort to dam up the laughter that was obviously threatening. Successfully mastering a deadpan expression, he looked at Reilly and said, "What a lovely dress. It makes a statement without being ostentatious."

Dylan Harrison was a good man with a wicked sense of humor—something Reilly was finding hard to appreciate at the moment. He wouldn't have put it past Alaina's husband to try kissing the back of his hand. Fuming, he sat back in his chair, crossed his arms over his padded bosom, tucking his knuckles safely out of harm's way. He squared one long leg over the other and scowled.

Dylan raised an eyebrow at the show of skin. "Time to break out the depilatory, Aunt Patty," he said dryly.

Reilly growled a stream of profanity under his breath as he uncrossed his hairy legs, pressed his knees together, and tugged down the hem of his dress.

"This isn't your usual crowd," Jayne commented, looking around at the rough and rowdy types bellying up to the bar and occupying the tables around them. She recognized a number of the reporters and fans scattered throughout who had been dogging Reilly's heels.

"Well, you know, the Loggerhead is temporarily closed due to a severe banana slug infestation, so we're catching the overflow."

"Is that good or bad?"

Dylan winced at the sound of raised voices and glasses breaking. "That remains to be seen." He started backing toward the bar. "Catch you later, Jayne." He grinned at Reilly. "Nice meeting you, Aunt Patty."

"Smart aleck," Reilly said with a snarl.

"You know," Jayne said, leaning closer to Reilly once more, "this is really an excellent opportunity for us. We can have a nice evening together without sexual overtones clouding our attempts to get to know each other better."

"What a lota rubbish," Reilly grumbled. "It seems to me we were doing just fine *with* the overtones. In fact, I rather enjoyed the overtones."

"Me, too," Jayne admitted. "It's just that everything's happening so fast—"

"This has been brewin' for some time, Jaynie, and you damn well know it."

"Yes, but—"

"But, what?" he questioned sharply. "I thought we agreed—no regrets."

Jayne squirmed a little in her chair. "I'm not having regrets—"

"You're having second thoughts."

"I'm having a heck of time finishing a sentence," she said, glaring at him.

Reilly refused to apologize. "I know you're ticked off because of the reporters and all that, but it's not my fault—"

"Not your fault?" she asked with an incredulous snort. "They didn't come here for the beaches and the fresh sea air."

"No, they didn't," he admitted, frustration goading him close to the edge of prudence. "They came here because I'm a star, and you can't handle that, can you, Jaynie?"

Jayne stared at him, taken aback. "What do you mean?"

Reilly cursed himself. He'd really put his foot in it now, but there was no going back. They were going to have to have this conversation sooner or later. "I mean, when you were with Mac, his world revolved around you. There were no interruptions. I've got other people to answer to, and you don't like it."

"You're saying I'm jealous?" she asked in disbelief.

"I'm saying you're scared," Reilly corrected her. He would be lucky if she didn't punch him in the nose for this, but it needed saying, and he believed in speaking the truth whenever it was possible. "The minute you start feeling overwhelmed, you back away and become a little mouse in the corner, watching instead of doing."

Jayne sat back in her chair and stared at him, unconsciously lending credence to Reilly's impulsively spoken words.

"That's probably why you're wasting your time being a critic instead of directing—"

"Now, wait just a darn minute—" Jayne began, only to be interrupted by the waitress, who plunked a tall drink down in front of her. She touched the little paper parasol sticking up out of the thing with a hesitant finger, then looked up at the waitress. "I didn't order this."

"Courtesy of the—er—gentleman at the end of the bar."

Wide-eyed, Jayne followed the waitress's nod. At the end of the bar sat a man who looked big enough to fell sequoias with his bare hands. She could only imagine how many yards of wool flannel it had taken to fashion the shirt he wore; enough to clothe a family of four, she guessed. His face could have fit in with the stone masks of Mount Rushmore, except that his was smiling with blatant male interest. He winked at her, and she jumped as if she'd been pinched.

"How sweet," she murmured weakly, sending him a tepid smile of thanks.

"Sweet?" Reilly said in a choked voice. Every jealous molecule in him snapped to attention and focused on the bugger who had dared send Jayne a drink. Beneath his pancake makeup, Reilly flushed ruby red, the color creeping up from beneath his lace collar to his face and spreading clear to his ears. He sat up straighter in his chair, his left hand unconsciously squeezing his pink purse.

Jayne's attention was on the large logger who

had pushed away from the bar and was swaggering toward their table. With a twist of his hairy wrist he turned the empty chair around and straddled it. Crossing his arms over the back of it, he lowered his head and spoke to Jayne in a voice that rumbled like an earthquake.

"Hi there, little lady. Mind if I sit down?" Jayne gulped.

"Is that a rhetorical question?"

His expression went blank for a second, then he dismissed her query and stuck out a hand the size of Montana. "Lloyd LaCroix."

Ingrained Southern manners made Jayne's response automatic. She gave two of his fingers a vigorous shake. "I'm Jayne Jordan and this is my Aunt Patty."

The lumberjack's gaze strayed absently toward Reilly. It was clearly his intention to simply nod a greeting and turn back to Jayne, but he did a double take instead. Looking startled, he said to Jayne, "Not much of a family resemblance, is there?"

"Oh, Aunt Patty is my mother's adopted sister," Jayne improvised. "Her folks were real poor and just couldn't feed all the kids, so one Sunday in church they asked other members of the congregation to take them in. Isn't that the saddest thing you ever heard?"

Lloyd LaCroix merely stared at her as if he hadn't counted on her being able to speak. On her other side, Jayne could feel the fury rolling off Reilly in waves of steam.

"And the strangest thing is," she went on, hoping Lloyd would get bored and wander off before things turned ugly, "Aunt Patty ended up marrying my daddy's Uncle Duke from Knob Lick. He ran a filling station down there and once sheared off his left pinky changing a fan belt on a pickup truck."

"That's real interesting," Lloyd said impatiently. "What do you say we talk about it some more later on? At my place."

Jayne winced.

Reilly was halfway across the table in the blink of an eye, his fist wrapping into the logger's shirt front. "What do you say you take your ugly mug out of the lady's face, mate?" he said in a voice several octaves too low to go with his outfit.

At LaCroix's startled look Jayne tried for an explanation that would salvage their ruse. "Aunt Patty's taking hormone treatments for her thyroid condition." She turned a plaintive look on Reilly. "Now, Aunt Patty you know how edgy that testosterone makes you. Lloyd here was only trying to be nice."

"Nice?" Reilly spat out the word. "I know all about what Lloyd here was tryin' to be."

"Look lady, I don't need this," LaCroix said, his eyes darting from Reilly to Jayne. "I'm plenty interested in you, but the ugly auntie here will have to take a hike."

Jayne jerked back as Reilly swung the pink handbag around and hit Lloyd on the side of the head with it. "I'll show you, you ugly, dirt-eatin' son of a sheepdog."

It was a classic example of all hell breaking loose, Jayne thought as she grabbed the knapsack she called a purse and scrambled to safety behind the bar. Reilly dove across the table, toppling Lloyd over backward. The lumberjack shoved at his attacker, swearing a blue streak. It was a sight to behold with awe and a certain amount of disgust: a lumberjack and a big ugly woman wrestling on the floor of the bar. A table of tabloid reporters leaped to the edge of the fray, snapping pictures from every angle. Around the melee people were cheering wildly, screaming and taking bets.

The odds changed considerably when Reilly's wig came off as the two men rolled across the floor. He hauled Lloyd to his feet and held him at arm's length. "Try to make off with my girl, will you?"

"You're a *man*!" the logger exclaimed, his face

a mask of repugnance. His horrified gaze swept down the length of Reilly's dress and back. "I've seen your kind on *Donahue*. It's because of sick guys like you that the Japanese are kicking our industrial butts!"

Reilly took exception, momentarily forgetting he was dressed for a mother-daughter tea. No one insulted his masculinity and got away with it. He took a swing at the lumberjack that landed squarely on the big man's chin, and the fight was on again. Punches flew fast and furious.

Jayne watched in horror. Her stomach churned at the thought of Reilly getting hurt. It was all her fault this was happening. And what was she doing about it? She was standing a safe distance back, watching—just as Reilly had accused her of doing. Observing instead of participating. Reilly was in danger of getting the spit kicked out of him, and she was taking it all in as if it were a scene in a movie!

She hopped up on the bar just as the two fighters stumbled in that direction. Reilly had a split lip and a bruise on his cheek, and his mascara was running, but he was holding his own. Still, Lloyd was bigger and possibly meaner. The odds didn't seem at all even to Jayne. As the men staggered closer, she swung her enormous purse with all her might, aiming for the back of LaCroix's head. She caught Reilly in the jaw as LaCroix dropped to the floor like a ton of bricks, felled by Reilly's best punch. Reilly went down, perpendicular to the logger, stunned by Jayne's blow.

"Oh, no!" Jayne exclaimed, sailing off the bar and dropping to her knees beside him. She stroked his cheek as he sat up, shaking his head to clear it. He rubbed his jaw, moving it gingerly to see that it wasn't broken. "I'm so sorry, honey!"

"What have you got in that bag, Jaynie, bricks?"

Jayne nibbled her thumbnail, tears rising in her eyes. "Reilly, this is no time to make jokes."

"Reilly!" The name went through the crowd like wildfire. It seemed the word was barely off Jayne's lips when the tabloid reporters pushed their way to the front of the mob, flashes popping.

"How long have you been cross-dressing, Reilly?"

"When did you decide to come out of the closet?"

Reilly heaved a sigh at the thought of the headlines that would be cluttering up next week's grocery checkout counters. Ignoring the questions the reporters were hurling at him, he looked at Jayne.

"So much for this disguise. Got any more bright ideas, Calamity Jayne?"

NINE

"Don't say it. Not one word, Patrick Reilly."

Reilly rubbed a hand across the grin splitting his handsome face. He winced as he bumped his split lip, but the brief sting of pain didn't distract him from the sight that had him ready to bust out laughing.

Jayne stood tugging ineffectually at the lead rope that was attached to her llama's halter. She was decked out in another of her crazy outfits. The full cotton skirt that hung nearly to her booted ankles was khaki with big pink and burgundy cabbage roses and dark green leaves. Her blouse was khaki as well, and fastened at the throat with an enormous cameo pin. On her head she wore a wide-brimmed army-green felt hat that looked at least a size too big for her. In short,

Reilly thought with a sense of wonder, she looked beautiful. It didn't make sense, but then, neither did Jayne most of the time. He loved her anyway.

In addition to her unique hiking attire, she wore an adorable little scowl, which she now turned on her obstinate llama. Pinafore patently ignored her mistress with the ethereal disregard unique to llamas. The animal sat on the trail like a big dog, gazing serenely off at the lovely view, craning her long neck this way and that in an effort to take it all in. She chewed placidly on the leaves she had snatched off a trailside bush just prior to plunking herself down.

"Did anyone ever tell her she's supposed to be a pack animal?" Reilly questioned. "She don't seem to be gettin' the point."

Jayne glared at him, frustrated and on the verge of tears. "You're some big help, you are, Mr. Macho Sheep Rancher."

Reilly shrugged. "That's no sheep, luv."

His heart melted as Jayne turned back to her llama to try once again to convince the recalcitrant animal to get up. She was taking Pinafore's reluctance personally, frowning at the llama in a way that clearly revealed her feelings of betrayal. She was so darn cute, he couldn't help but want to wrap her up in his arms and kiss her senseless.

Hiking into the rugged, wooded hills of her farm had been Jayne's second bright idea designed to extract them from reporters and fans. It had sounded like a good plan to Reilly—until she had insisted they take two llamas along with them to carry their gear. There had been no dissuading her. Sweet-natured though she was, Jayne had a stubborn streak in her not even Reilly could break. So they had strapped packs on Pinafore and Jodhpur, loaded them with food and Jayne's brand-spanking new camping gear, and headed for the hills just as the sun was peeking over the far horizon.

The plan had worked. There wasn't a reporter in sight. Reilly was pretty sure they had lost the press in the fog somewhere along the coastal highway after the incident in the bar. Candi had thrown them farther off the track by telling all callers that Jayne had gone to L.A. for the weekend to visit old friends.

Now Reilly adjusted the brim of his hat and breathed deeply the pine-scented air. He sighed a sigh of supreme contentment. This was beautiful country. Rough and wooded, thick with verdant plant life and wildlife. It would be easy for a man to lose himself in it, to forget there was a world full of pressures waiting just to the west of these hills. That was exactly what he planned to do—just as soon as he rescued Jayne from the clutches of her evil llama.

He gave a shrill whistle that brought Rowdy to his side, then sent the dog to bark at the reluctant pack animal. The sheepdog glared at his master, obviously put out at being asked to herd a lowly llama. Rowdy gave a couple of obligatory barks, then joined Pinafore in her boycott of the trip. He sat down with his back to the llama, and stared off at the countryside.

"You're losin' your touch," Reilly grumbled to the dog.

Rowdy ignored him.

Disgusted with the whole business, Jayne threw her lead rope down and stamped her dainty feet. She shook her finger at Reilly.

"This is all your fault! You and your blasted pack of rabid disciples! I had a perfectly nice life until you showed up. Now look what's happened! I've been chased out of my home, my bracelet isn't working, I can't communicate with my llama, and I don't know where the center of the earth is!"

"Bloody hell," Reilly grumbled with half a grin, trying to keep things light. The prospect of a crying woman made him shudder in his boots. "You make me sound like a walking holocaust."

"You are." Jayne hiccupped as she tried valiantly to keep from bursting into tears.

She was at the end of her rope. They had been walking for three hours. Three hours of rancid llama breath down the back of her neck. Three hours of llama humming in her ear. Three hours of stopping every two miles to coax Pinafore off her fluffy duff. Three hours of pointless introspection.

Her feet were sore inside her new hiking boots, and her feelings were rubbed raw. The tension of the past few weeks had come to a head; she felt as if something in her chest was going to explode if she didn't sort it all out soon. There were her own feelings of uncertainty regarding Reilly and what he ultimately would want in a relationship. There was confusion at the lack of spiritual guidance she was receiving from her heretofore trusty bracelet. There was the conflict between her view of her life and Reilly's vastly different interpretation of it.

All she had ever wanted was a place where she fit in, a place where she would know security and peace and bliss—the kinds of feelings she had

known within the ranks of the Fearsome Foursome back at college, the kinds of feelings she had
known with Mac. How was she ever going to find
those things with a man who made her feel as if
she were caught up in a hurricane?

"What do you mean your bracelet isn't working?" Reilly asked, latching on to the one problem she had mentioned that sounded solvable. He
abandoned his llama in favor of putting his arms
around Jayne, gathering her against him in a gentle embrace. "What's the matter? Is the latch broken? Maybe I can fix it."

"Fix it?" Jayne chuckled wearily to herself.
"How can you fix it? You're the problem."

Reilly raised a brow and tucked his square chin
back defensively. "Me? I haven't touched the
thing. You never take it off."

His big hand gently circled her left arm and
raised it so he could easily examine the bracelet. It
seemed perfectly intact to him. The gold of the in-
tricately woven chain shown dully in the morning
light. The dainty key charm lay against the paper-
thin skin inside Jayne's wrist.

"Looks fine to me," he said, his voice going a
little hoarse at the feel of Jayne's pulse racing beneath his thumb.

Jayne heaved a sigh of premature defeat. She

could already hear Reilly declaring her belief to be bunk. Still, she felt obligated to explain.

"This bracelet was a gift from Bryan. He bought it from a gypsy in Hungary who told him it had powers, that the key was the key to a plane of understanding. But I haven't been able to understand anything since you've shown up. Do you follow so far?"

Scowling, Reilly tilted his hat back and scratched his head, the picture of male confusion. "Not a bit of it."

"This bracelet has always given me feelings—good or bad—that help me make decisions," she said, trying to convince him with her earnest expression as well as her heartfelt words. "It hasn't done a darn thing since you came here. I think your magnetism has goofed up the psychic energy field. I can't get any idea of what to do about you or anything else."

Reilly stared at her for a long moment, his face frozen in a look of dismayed disbelief. Dropping her hand, he took two steps back from her and barked a sharp laugh that turned the heads of both llamas. He threw his hands up in utter exasperation. "What a lota rubbish, Jaynie!"

Jayne squeezed her eyes shut and sighed again.

She might as well have been talking to the llamas. Come to think of it, they probably had a better understanding of the mystical world than Reilly did, llamas being such soulful creatures.

"I knew you wouldn't understand," she muttered, feeling the rift between them widening.

"Oh, I understand plenty," Reilly said, coming back to her with his hands jammed at the waistband of his faded jeans. He leaned over her, trying to intimidate her with his size and his scowl. He'd had it with Jayne's metaphysical malarkey. She was scared, and her reaction was to hold up that shield of mystical mumbo-jumbo, but he wasn't having any of it. "I understand that there's something burning between us that's worth hanging on to, and no bloody bit of junk jewelry is gonna tell me different."

He pushed her hat back off her head and roughly stroked a hand over the luxuriant, wild mass of her hair, tilting her head back with the pressure.

"Look at me, Jaynie," he commanded.

She had no choice but to obey him. Staring up into the burning opalescent intensity of his eyes, she shivered at the raw sensual feelings that stirred inside her. He was so utterly masculine; every feminine instinct in her snapped to attention when he came this close. The sensation was powerful, overwhelming, frightening.

"Do you love me?" he demanded. The expression on his rugged, irregular features would have dissuaded more than one woman from answering.

Jayne's heart did a back flip. Her dark eyes widened impossibly in a pixie face gone suddenly pale. Did she love him? Stupid man. Hadn't he been paying any attention to her at all? Everybody in Anastasia knew she was in love with him!

"Well, do you?"

His voice was sure and strong, but there was less certainty in his blue eyes. He wasn't asking just to hear the sound of his own voice. That hint of vulnerability caught at Jayne's heart and gave her the courage to answer with the truth.

"Yes," she whispered, sliding her hands up inside his leather jacket, along the hard planes of a chest covered in soft red cotton.

Reilly studied her with an intensity that bordered on fanaticism. He took in not only her admission, but her expression, the thread of hesitancy in her voice, the square set of her shoulders as if she were tensed to receive a blow of some kind.

She was scared. He was shaking the foundation of her world and she didn't like it. But she loved him. That was all he needed to hear for the moment. They would deal with the rest later.

"All right, then," he said with a nod and a satisfied sigh. "Stop backing away from it."

He kissed her soundly, then turned and started toward the obdurate Pinafore.

Jayne stared after him, slack-jawed. She felt as if she'd been knocked senseless. Her head was swimming. Reilly had just bullied an admission of love out of her and calmly walked away as if nothing earth-shattering had happened at all!

"Reilly!"

"Shake a leg, sheila," he said, tossing her a glance as he scooped up Pinafore's lead rope. He tugged down the brim of his hat and stared off down the trail that led north and east. "We're burnin' daylight."

He clucked to the llama. Pinafore immediately stood and stretched, then looked off down the trail as if to tell everyone she was more than ready to leave.

Reilly grinned and winked at Jayne's look of outraged disbelief. "Guess I've just got a way with the ladies."

Jayne bit her lip on her retort. She didn't want to think about Reilly's way with the ladies. Uncertainty swirled inside her like a chilly wind. She was on the brink of giving her heart to a man who had a reputation for whipping women into a sexual frenzy with nothing more than a casual glance.

But it wasn't as if he encouraged them, was it? As she plodded down the trail with Jodhpur breathing down her neck, she thought back on all that had happened since Reilly had come to Anastasia. He could have stayed in L.A. and soaked up the publicity from the *WE* article, but he hadn't. When the press and his fans had discovered his whereabouts, he could have leaped into the limelight and let them lavish their attention on him, but he hadn't. All he had asked for from the start was to have some time to spend with her, Jayne Jordan.

Her heart warmed at the thought as she took Jodhpur's rope and started down the trail after Pinafore and Reilly.

Maybe Reilly was right. Maybe she was simply feeling overwhelmed, and her natural reaction was to back away. Maybe this had nothing to do with the fact that her bracelet wasn't working. Maybe this was about going after something she wanted, following a rainbow, and claiming the treasure at the end of it.

She ignored the niggling doubt in the back of her mind. Reilly had accused her of being an observer of life rather than a participant in it. Well, she had him all to herself now, and she was darn well going to participate, she thought as she focused a purposeful gaze on his back.

They stopped for lunch in a sun-dappled glade beside a clear stream. All around them towered the redwood trees the area was known for. Nearer the ground, ferns and other lush green growth spread out in an edible carpet the llamas found irresistible. Rowdy found a sunny spot to curl up and nap in. Reilly plunked their food pack down on a rock and began rummaging through it in search of a sandwich.

"Hungry?" Jayne asked in the most sultry voice she could conjure up, concentrating on memories of old Lauren Bacall movies.

"I'll say. I'm so hungry I could eat—" The words stuck in Reilly's throat as he glanced over his broad shoulder at Jayne.

She stood no more than five feet behind him, her burnished dark hair loose and lifting around her shoulders on the slight breeze. Her dark eyes were glowing with sensual promise. Her dainty fingers were slowly undoing the buttons on her blouse. The vee of exposed skin reached almost to her tummy.

"I'm hungry, too," she murmured, her gaze

locked on his. She paused for just the right effect and added, "For you."

Reilly's hormones bolted to life with a speed that was nearly painful. Want of Jayne was something he had learned to live with. Thankfully, it was no longer something he had to deny. Forgetting all about the sandwiches, his full attention focused on the woman before him, and he smiled with a sense of anticipation and wonder.

Jayne had never played the seductress with him. He had always initiated their lovemaking. In fact, over the past couple of weeks he had sensed a certain reluctance in her. He had felt her pulling away because of all the attention he was getting from the paparazzi and his fans. But now Jayne was clearly assuming the role of the aggressor. Reilly wondered dimly if it had anything to do with their being isolated. If it did, he decided as Jayne slid her blouse back off her shoulders and let it drop, he was going to chuck it all and become a hermit.

"What are you doing, Jaynie?" he questioned softly as she lifted her hands to his shirt front and began to slip the buttons from their moorings.

"You told me to stop backing away," she said.

"Mmm . . ." He sighed as she pulled his shirt-tails from his jeans. "What about the llamas?"

"They won't bother us," she said, dragging the red shirt back off his broad shoulders, baring his chest to her gaze and her kisses. She brushed her lips over his skin and delighted in the scent and taste of him. Wild shivers coursed through her. Participating in life was fun, worrying wasn't. That particular philosophy was gaining popularity with her in direct proportion to the increasing intensity of her desire. "I told them to take a nap after lunch."

"And you're not worried about them being your maiden aunts come back to life in hairy animal hides?"

Jayne broke off from her exploration of his chest to give him a narrow look. "I'm trying to seduce you here, Reilly. Would you mind just keeping your mouth shut for once?"

"No problem," he said, fighting a grin. "But isn't that gonna make it hard for me to kiss you?"

"Good point," Jayne conceded, fighting an attack of giggles. She wound her arms around his neck and lifted herself against him, pressing her bare breasts to the sun-warmed planes of his chest. The contact was delicious, and it sent the last of her doubts scattering. Nothing ever seemed wrong when she was in Reilly's arms. All their differences in personality and life philosophy just melted away. All the distractions and demands of his profession disappeared. There was only the two of them and the love that was struggling to come to life between them.

She arched against him like a cat and nipped at the cleft in his chin. "So kiss me, you aggravating Aussie."

"With pleasure," Reilly murmured, tilting his head and lowering it toward hers.

It was a sweet kiss. A kiss full of welcome and relief. Reilly gathered Jayne up against him and reveled in the feel of her in his arms. This was what he wanted, this sense of peace and contentment he knew only with Jayne. It was something that his career denied him. It was something he could no longer depend upon his family for. Only Jayne gave him this haven. It didn't matter that she could be a complete flake. It didn't matter that she kept a tarantula and thought her jewelry spoke to her. She was the woman who believed in him. She was the woman he loved.

He lowered her to the blanket of clothes they had dropped on the ground. The clean, fertile scents of the forest filled his head, but overriding it was Jayne's soft perfume. He buried his face between her breasts and drank the fragrance in, intoxicating himself with it. Trailing kisses from one taut nipple to the other, he sipped at the sweet taste of her, then took his mouth to hers and drank in the wine of her kiss.

Jayne was filled with a pure joy unlike anything she'd ever experienced. She felt like Eve. Alone there with Reilly in the middle of the forest, it was as if they were the only people on earth. It seemed only right that they shed their clothing and were celebrating the wonders of life and love and nature.

She gazed at Reilly, poised above her. He was the perfect example of the male of the species—strong, ruggedly masculine, handsome in a way that wasn't quite civilized. She stroked her hand down his chest and across his quivering belly to the most masculine part of him. With her gaze locked on his, her small fingers closed around his shaft and guided him to her.

They both gasped at the first touch of flesh to flesh. The gasps segued to groans as male hardness slid into the welcoming warmth of feminine silk. The groans trailed off into sighs at the first sensation of completion. They savored their union, kissing and touching and murmuring words of love. Then need urged them off the first plateau and made them reach for a higher one.

Reilly reached his climax first, clutching Jayne

to him as the explosion rocked him, blinding him to everything else except bliss. When the tremors subsided, he rolled onto his back and urged Jayne to take her own pleasure. He watched as she moved on him, her every expression crossing her face like scenes on a movie screen.

She was so open, so honest in her lovemaking, simply watching her aroused him all over again. Gripping her slender waist with his big hands, he lifted his hips to meet her as she slid down on him.

Jayne groaned Reilly's name over and over, faster and faster, in time with their movements, until the tension coiling inside her burst, flooding her with fulfillment and love. Exhausted, she collapsed on his chest, her cheek pressing against his sweat-dampened skin.

Reilly wrapped his arms around her and pressed soft kisses to the top of her head. Lazily, Jayne traced patterns on his chest with her finger, her gaze fixed on the small gold key that dangled from her wrist and dragged along, catching in Reilly's chest hairs.

This seemed so perfect. Why wasn't her faithful source confirming that feeling?

"Are you happy now that you've had your way

with me?" Reilly asked, his voice at once soft and rough, like corduroy.

Jayne jerked her head around to look at him. Lord, he was sexy. His golden hair was tousled, his eyes were dark with sated passion. He looked perfectly at home, naked in the woods. She gave him a sassy look.

"Maybe I'm not finished with you yet."

"Don't let me rush you," he said, stroking a hand down the supple line of her back and over the curve of her buttock. He pulled her tighter against his groin and groaned as her body responded by tightening around him. "I'm in no hurry."

Propping herself up on his chest with one arm, Jayne reached up and brushed at the bits of greenery that clung to his hair. Her expression turned wistful. "I wish it could always be like this."

Reilly didn't have to ask what she meant. He would have wished it too, but it didn't seem sensible. "We both have lives to lead, Jaynie," he said softly, almost regretfully. "We've got jobs to do and people to answer to. We can't shut the world out, and we can't just watch it go by."

"I'm not just watching," Jayne said in protest. Hurt, she pulled away from him and collected what clothing she could without trying to move

Reilly. She jerked her blouse on and began fastening buttons. "I'm involved in life around Anastasia. I started the theater group. I took Candi in. I resent your saying I don't do anything but watch. You make me sound like a voyeur."

"Aw, Jaynie, that's not what I mean at all." He sat up and pulled her back into his arms, ignoring her struggles to escape. He gave her a squeeze to still her, then pressed a kiss to her temple. "I just mean we can't always have the world to ourselves. You don't like the way the press intruded on our time. I don't like it either, but that's part of my life. As much as I'd love to stay in these hills with you, I have other obligations. I'll have to go down to L.A. next week for the opening of *Deadly Intent*."

Jayne felt a chill go through her like a knife. "What about the play?"

"What about it? I'll miss one rehearsal. My understudy can walk through it." He released her and began sorting through the rumpled, squished pile of clothes around him. Dismissing the topic of conversation, he stood up and pulled on his briefs and jeans.

Jayne watched him, absently finishing dressing, her fingers fastening buttons and snaps while her brain concentrated on the horrible sensation of dread that was suddenly filling her stomach. "You'll be back for opening night?"

Reilly pulled an athletic sock off a bush and gave Jayne a strange look as he pulled it on. "Course I'll be back."

"Why didn't you tell me about this sooner?"

He shrugged as he pulled his shirt on. "Slipped my mind, I guess," he muttered.

"It slipped your mind?" Jayne's voice rang with disbelief. "You've got a multimillion-dollar movie coming out next week and it slipped your mind?"

"All right," he conceded with a frustrated sigh. "Maybe I didn't want to talk about *Deadly Intent* because I didn't want to get another lecture from you on how I'm wastin' my talent on movies that don't mean anything."

Jayne nibbled on her thumbnail and said nothing. What could she say? If *Deadly Intent* proved to be anything like its predecessors, then it had indeed been a waste of Reilly's considerable talents. But she also knew he'd had his reasons for choosing the scripts he had. She couldn't fault him for being loyal to his family and his friends.

"Truth to tell, it never slipped my mind," Reilly mumbled, jamming his shirttail into his jeans. "The director is a pal of mine. He owns a piece of the film, and he needs the thing to do big at the box office."

Jayne listened, torn between love and suspicion. She loved the man who made sacrifices for the people he cared about. She was suspicious of the actor who dropped this kind of information ever so skillfully on the ears of a prominent film critic. And she hated herself for her doubts. She wished with all her might for some kind of sign to assure her that Pat Reilly wouldn't play on her sympathies, then blithely break her heart. She hooked two fingers through the chain of her bracelet, hoping against hope for some special feeling, but nothing happened.

Reilly caught the action and frowned. He didn't like the way Jayne took such stock in things like premonitions and karma and all that other crap, but her convictions were a vital part of who she was. A man had to take the bad with the good, he supposed. And there was a lot of good in his Jaynie.

"No more talkin' business," he declared, closing the distance between them and dropping a kiss on Jayne's downturned lips. "We're not likely to agree on it, and that's that. We came up here to enjoy the scenery and each other. So," he said, flashing her his famous Cheshire-cat smile, "if you've enjoyed me enough for the moment, we can hit the trail, Calamity Jayne."

Jayne looked up at him, trying her best to shake the heavy mood that was pressing down on her chest like a stone. "I love you," she said, needing to hear the words. She managed a tiny scrap of a smile. "You're obnoxious, but I love you."

"That's what I like to hear," Reilly said sardonically as he pulled on his hat. "Flattery."

True to his word, Reilly didn't mention business again that day. While Jayne couldn't stop part of her brain from worrying and wondering, she did her best to ignore it and to immerse herself in the experience of camping in beautiful surroundings with the man she loved. She threw herself wholeheartedly into the spirit of the great outdoors, even though it was readily apparent she knew nothing about camping and wasn't particularly outdoorsy.

"I don't understand why you bought all this campin' gear, luv," Reilly said, gesturing with his tin coffee cup to the dome-shaped tent and other paraphernalia. "I dare say, you're not cut out for the pioneer life."

He was stretched out on his side near the campfire. Twilight was closing in around them. Jayne's heart beat a little harder while she was looking at him. He seemed so relaxed, so within his element. It was another difference between them, but not one that bothered her overmuch. She was glad to see Reilly spiritually centered and at peace with himself.

She took a sip of the tea she had brewed for herself, resolutely refusing to acknowledge, even to herself, how bad it was. "I figured I could learn. I wanted to commune with the true spirits of nature."

For once, Reilly didn't try to argue with her. "It's a beautiful place to do that," he said wistfully. "It's kinda like home in some ways."

"Do you miss Australia?" Jayne asked, the note of homesickness in his voice catching at her heart.

"Some," he admitted, thinking about the sheep station, his family, and old friends. The memories were good, but he knew nothing would be the same if he tried to go back. People looked at him differently now, expected different things of him than they had when he'd been his father's foreman. There was too much truth in the old saw that says you can't go home again, he thought sadly. "My life is here now, in the States."

He almost added "with you," but he didn't think this was the time to push. Jayne had been too skittish of late. Besides, he had it all planned out, the when and the where. There were details that needed to fall into place before he would feel ready to make Jayne his for good.

He tossed the last of his coffee onto the dying fire, stood up, and stretched. "It's been a long day, luv. Let's turn in."

Jayne eyed the tent and nibbled on her thumbnail. She said nothing as they put the fire out and checked on the animals. But when Reilly opened the tent flap and motioned for her to precede him inside, she balked. Old fears sprang to life inside her and panic grabbed at her throat. She made one attempt to go inside the little blue nylon dome, but shot back out the instant her head was between the panels of the door.

"I can't," she whispered, so embarrassed she couldn't even look at Reilly. Tears sprang up in her luminous dark eyes. "I'm sorry. I thought I could, but I can't."

"Jaynie, what is it?" he asked with genuine concern. He dropped the tent flap and coaxed Jayne into his embrace. She was trembling.

"You'll laugh," Jayne said dismally.

"I won't, I promise. You know I always keep my promises."

Silent, Jayne hugged him. He might think she was a kook, but he'd said he wouldn't laugh, and she believed him. "I'm claustrophobic," she admitted in a tiny voice. "I thought I could handle the tent because it's outside and all, but . . ."

Claustrophobic, Reilly thought as he stroked a hand over the wild tangle of Jayne's hair. That explained the enormous house that was all windows and no walls. It also explained the huge bed that had no headboard or footboard. It probably explained her convertible car as well.

"I accidentally got locked in a closet once when I was little," Jayne explained, shuddering at the memory. "You think it's silly for me to still be afraid, I know, just like you think my beliefs in karma and auras are silly."

"I don't think you're silly. Not about this, anyway," he said. He gave her a gentle smile when she scowled at him. "I know what it's like to be afraid, luv. I know what it is to need a friend's support. I dare say we're friends."

Tears of love flooded Jayne's eyes. He could be a truly wonderful man. "Best friends," she said with a smile of gratitude.

Reilly dropped a kiss on the tip of her nose and winked. "Wait here."

Without another word, he went into the tent and dragged out the down-filled double sleeping bag and the pillows, arranged them where they would have the best view of the last colors of twilight and the moon hanging high above the horizon in the dark part of the sky. When he opened his arms in invitation, Jayne went willingly and snuggled against him.

"Are you sure you don't mind not using the tent?"

Reilly made a face. "Who needs a tent? You can't see the stars from inside a tent, now, can you?"

Jayne's only reply was to hug him. As long as she had Reilly nearby, she thought, she would always be able to see a star.

TEN

SOMETHING TERRIBLE WAS going to happen.

Jayne shuddered as the belief surged through her again. It had first descended on her in the middle of the night. She had awakened from a disturbing dream, sitting bolt upright and jerking half the sleeping bag up with her. An icy fear had lodged itself in the center of her chest, radiating waves of aching cold through her, down her arms and legs. But the most conclusive evidence had been her bracelet.

The gold links had pressed warmly to her skin, the key hanging from it with the weight of an anchor. After weeks of lying dormant, the power within it had finally come to life. Jayne had hooked two fingers through the chain, and shivered as the premonition came to her.

Something terrible was going to happen.

It was a horrible burden to know that and not tell anyone. Had she been home she would have shared the news with Bryan; he would have understood her concern, at least. But she couldn't tell Reilly. Reilly didn't believe in premonitions. He lived in blissful ignorance of that other plane of understanding, the lucky bugger.

When he had awakened and asked her what was wrong, she'd told him she'd had a bad dream. His solution had been to make long, slow, passionate love to her. Not a bad distraction, she had to admit, but hardly the answer she needed.

It was depressing. After a lovely day of forgetting about the rest of the world, of drinking in the scenery and making love with Reilly, this black premonition had descended and ruined everything. She had spent the morning wondering about the meaning of it all. Why did her life path seem destined to collide with Reilly's only to part? What did their karmas ultimately have in store for them?

Now, as they trudged west in ominous silence toward her farm, Jayne hooked her fingers through the bracelet again, and again felt that horrible shiver of anticipation. She didn't know what.

She didn't know when. She didn't know where. But something terrible was going to happen.

"That does it," Reilly said, temper clipping his words apart. He stopped in his tracks, yanking his hat off and throwing it down on the ground in frustration.

Pinafore promptly sat down. Rowdy gave one aggravated bark, then dropped down on the ground and put his head on his paws.

Jayne pulled Jodhpur to a halt and turned wide eyes on Reilly. "What?"

"What?" He huffed an irritated sigh, his dark golden brows riding low over eyes that were as blue as the sky. He hitched his hands to the waistband of his jeans, hunching his shoulders aggressively. "You've been goin' around all day twistin' at that bloody chain, lookin' like the end of the world was at hand. I want to know why. What's goin' on here, Jaynie?"

Jayne cast a guilty look at her wrist and the two fingers she had wound into the bracelet. She let go of the chain and scratched at her forearm. "Nothing," she said. It sounded more like a question than an answer.

"We had a nice time together this weekend, didn't we?" Reilly said in a tone of voice that dared her to say otherwise.

She nodded.

"Then what's goin' on here? You're too quiet by half." He narrowed his eyes in suspicion.

Jayne bridled at the remark and the look. She crossed her arms over the Notre Dame insignia on her navy-blue sweatshirt. "What's that supposed to mean?"

"It means the same thing it always means in the movies," Reilly said. "Trouble. So tell me now what you've got on your mind."

Looking away from him, she nibbled at her thumbnail and considered an out-and-out fib, but rejected the idea. Reilly had the bit in his teeth now. He wouldn't let go until she'd given him an answer. "I've just got a bad feeling, that's all."

"A bad feelin' about what?"

She shrugged.

Reining in his temper, Reilly closed the distance between them. He cupped Jayne's face with his hands and tilted it up so he could look into her big dark eyes. The uncertainty he saw there cut at his heart.

"We've got to have this out, Jaynie," he said gently. "I came up here to settle this thing between us. We won't get anywhere if you keep secrets. What is it you're so afraid of?"

"Settle it? You make it sound as if I'm some

kind loose end in a business deal," she said irritably. "Is that the only reason you came here, Reilly? To settle the past?"

"I made us both a promise, Jaynie." He paused, holding her gaze with his as the breeze swirled gently around them and tugged at the ends of Jayne's dark hair. "I don't regret keepin' it. Do you?"

"No," she answered automatically, but immediately she was assailed by doubts. "Yes." She squeezed her eyes shut and shook her head as if to clear it of Reilly's compelling image. When she opened them, she looked off to the west and murmured. "I don't know."

"You told me you loved me," Reilly said, doing his best to keep his own fears out of his voice. Jayne owned every corner of his heart. He didn't think he could stand the idea of her taking it back.

"I do love you," Jayne said earnestly. "I'm just not sure if that's a good thing."

Reilly let irritation override everything else he was feeling. He wasn't a patient man. He wanted Jaynie, body and soul, and he was getting tired of waiting for her. It seemed that was all he'd been doing for most of his adult life—waiting to have Jayne Jordan love him. Now she admitted loving him but was waffling on the issue.

"What the bloody hell is that supposed to

mean?" he asked, lifting his hands in a gesture of frustration that hinted at his desire to shake some sense into the silly woman. "Of course it's a good thing! People in love should be happy, dammit. Why aren't you?"

She could have pointed out that he didn't seem terribly overjoyed himself, but she refrained. That wasn't the issue. "Because something bad is going to happen," she said, bracing herself for a barrage of practical questions.

Reilly looked at her as if she'd suddenly begun speaking Greek. "What?"

"You want to know what's bothering me. Fine. I'll tell you, but you won't like it," she promised. "Something bad is going to happen. I can feel it. I can sense it."

Reilly's reply was vulgar and succinct, a two-syllable barnyard word that summed up his opinion of Jayne's penchant for premonitions and the like.

"What's gonna to happen?" he asked, challenging her to put her money where her mouth was. "When?"

"I don't know," Jayne admitted morosely. For all she knew, this was it. They weren't exactly having a jolly good time. But, somehow, she suspected this was just a tremor; the real earthquake was yet to come.

While the llamas looked on, Reilly paced back and forth in front of Jayne, reprising his role as the courtroom lawyer in *Malice of Forethought.* "How do you know this bad thing is gonna happen?"

All Jayne had to do was glance at her left wrist, and Reilly went off, his ready temper exploding like a Roman candle. He grabbed hold of her wrist and jerked her hand up. The tiny gold key glittered prettily in the sun, oblivious to the trouble it was creating.

"I've had it with this bracelet," Reilly said through clenched teeth.

He hooked a finger between the gold chain and the fine skin on the inside of Jayne's wrist and gave a tug. Jayne gasped as the clasp of the bracelet gave. Reilly coiled his fist around the loose chain. The key and bracelet disappeared inside his big hand.

Jayne's expression was one of utter dismay as she stared at his fist. She hadn't taken that bracelet off since the day Bryan had given it to her. She felt naked without it. Worse, she felt cut adrift from a source of security.

Reilly tucked a finger beneath her chin and turned her head to meet his gaze.

"Jewelry can't see into the future, Jayne," he said in a dangerous tone. "Get that through your flaky head. What you're feeling is fear, pure and simple. Why don't you admit it? You had a nice borin' little life here until I came back. You could have gone forever coastin' along takin' in strays and watchin' the world go by. I've upset your apple cart, and you don't like it."

"No, I don't like it," she admitted, tears gathering in her eyes. "I told you that when you came here, but did it make any difference to you? No. You just went right ahead and made me fall in love with you anyway. And what will I have to show for it? Nothing, because you're going back to Hollywood!"

"It's just a premiere. I'll be back—" He cut himself off and swore under his breath as it hit him. "You think I won't come back. You don't trust me."

Jayne couldn't quite deny it. It wasn't that she didn't trust Reilly the man. She didn't trust Reilly the actor. They were two separate people to her. Unfortunately, they were wrapped up together in one devilishly handsome package. She didn't know what to say, so she said nothing.

Reilly backed away for a moment, trying to gather his thoughts. His pride was smarting. No one ever questioned his integrity. Where he came from, a man was as good as his word and that was that. Realizing Jayne didn't trust him was like taking a blow to his solar plexus. He could actually feel the dark bruise spread across his pride and his heart.

Once he'd gotten his breath back, he took up his stance in front of her again, planting his battered boots and squaring his broad shoulders, digging in for the duration of the fight. "I promise you I'll come back, Jaynie," he said. "I always keep my promises. You, of all people, should know that."

"I do." But she couldn't shake the fear that their relationship was in imminent danger, and that fear was more than apparent in her eyes as she looked up at him.

"You trust this bloody bracelet more than you trust me," Reilly murmured, opening his fist to stare in wonder at the dull gold links. He shook his head as he returned his attention to Jayne. "That's not the way it works, Jaynie. You love, you trust me. It's as simple as that."

Oh, she loved him. But there wasn't anything simple about it, Jayne thought. She longed for peace and contentment. Reilly was a whirlwind of burning intensity. She had been a challenge to him. He had conquered the challenge. She couldn't quite overcome the fear that he would now turn his intensity elsewhere. She had seen it happen time and again. She had had it happen.

How many times before she'd met Mac had she been courted by an actor only to be left when she couldn't pay homage to his ego? Now Reilly was heading back to Hollywood for the premiere of a movie she was almost certain to detest. She couldn't help but think this would be the crossroads where the paths of their lives would go in separate directions.

"You're afraid to really love me," Reilly said. "It was easy with Mac, wasn't it? His whole world revolved around you. It can't be hard to love someone who worships you. Don't get me wrong—I love you, Jaynie, but I'm not some tame old horse you can lead around by the nose. I've got responsibilities outside our relationship, whether you like it or not. But there's one thing you can always be sure of: I'll always come back."

Tangling his fist in her hair, he leaned down and pressed his lips to hers. His other arm banded around her and lifted her. Her body bent against his like a willow to an oak. For just an instant, Jayne tried to keep her spirit from yielding as well, but the attempt was futile. She could no more deny him this than she could deny the sun's rising. And, in truth, she didn't want to deny him. She wanted to drink in every drop of attention she could get from him. She wanted to bask in the burning flame of Reilly's desire, because she knew from experience how cold and alone she would be once he left.

So she gave him the kiss he demanded. She ran her hands back through the golden silk of his wind-tossed hair and over the smooth, soft leather of his old jacket. She pressed her palms to his cheeks and memorized the planes and angles of his lean face. She kissed him with all the love in her heart and sent up a prayer to the deities that, for once, the premonition the key had given her would prove false.

"Take a look at this," Candi said indignantly the instant Reilly and Jayne stepped into the house. She snapped a purple fingernail against the banner headline on the *Weekly Globe Report*. It read "Critic and Casanova: Match Made in Hollywood Heaven?"

"You guys made lead story with your vanishing act. You beat out 'I'm Having Elvis's Love Child.'"

Jayne did a double take, studying the small photo under the second, less prominent, headline as she took a seat at the kitchen table. She scowled at her young charge. "Candi, this is you!"

The teenager patted a hand to her newly dyed burgundy spiked hair and batted her black eyelids. "Nice picture, huh? I look like Tracey Ullman, don't you think?"

Reilly checked the photo and shrugged. "Kind of."

Jayne smacked his arm and swiveled her ornery look from him back across the table to Candi. "Elvis's love child?"

"And it didn't make the headline," the girl complained, deliberately ignoring Jayne's point. She picked up a Fig Newton and nibbled at one corner. "People got no respect for the King anymore."

"Oh, my Lord!" Jayne exclaimed as her attention was captured by the sentence beneath the banner headline. Her blood ran cold as she read it out loud. "'Reilly woos reviews as *Deadly Intent* is released.'"

It was one of her worst fears typed out in bold italics for all the gossip-mongering world to see. As much as she didn't want to believe it possible, she had been wooed for reviews before. And the fact remained, Reilly had deliberately avoided talking to her about the film—a classic misdirection maneuver designed to soften her up.

Her heart didn't want to believe he was the kind of man to stoop to such a trick, but her head kept reminding her of others who had been, and then there was the matter of her bracelet. Something terrible was going to happen.

Reilly made a rude sound and dismissed the article with a wave of his hand as if he were a king dismissing a declaration of war made against him by some puny principality. "Bloody rubbish. I wouldn't insult a parrot by linin' his cage with that rag. I don't know how many times I'll have to sue the buggers before they leave me alone."

"It's a good picture of you," Candi commented.

Jayne made a face as she studied the photo. It was of Reilly in a tux, looking devastating. He had his arm around a voluptuous female body in a skintight, black lace evening gown. Jayne's own face stared up at him, her head tilted at a weird angle.

Her jaw dropped open in outrage. "They stuck my head on Anna Jonsen's body!"

"Yeah," Candi said, cracking her gum. "You never dress that nice."

"This is terrible!" Jayne ranted. "My credibility could be destroyed by an article like this!"

"What credibility?" Reilly questioned sarcastically as he pulled a beer from the refrigerator and popped the top. "You're a critic."

"Go ahead, make jokes, Casanova," Jayne snapped, swatting at him with the paper. "I happen to take my job seriously."

"Bloody waste of time and talent," he said crossly, his temper rising.

Jayne rolled her eyes. "That's a good one. Take a look in the mirror the next time you say that. Ooooh," she moaned to herself, her brow knitting as she looked at the headline once more. "I knew something bad was going to happen. I just knew it."

Reilly swore, slamming his beer can down on the table. "This has nothing to do with that blasted bracelet."

"Before this gets really ugly, can I give you your messages?" Candi asked.

Reilly and Jayne turned on her simultaneously. "What?"

"Jeez," Candi muttered, wincing. "I think I was safer living on the streets." She picked up a notepad and cleared her throat. "Reilly, your publicist called and said you're supposed to be at the premiere tomorrow by seven. He's already arranged for a limo to pick you up at your place. Jayne, you're supposed to be in San Francisco tonight for a special screening of *Deadly Intent*." She bobbed her eyebrows and forced a toothy smile. "Nice timing, huh?"

"I'll drive down with you," Reilly said, his gaze riveted on Jayne.

It was not a suggestion. It was a dictate. Jayne shook her head, pressing her fingers to her temples where a sudden headache was drumming out a reggae beat. This was it. This was going to be the big one, the disaster her charm had foretold.

"You can't go to the screening with me, Reilly."

"I don't want to go to the screenin' with you. I said I'd drive down with you. You can drop me at the airport. I'll catch an evenin' flight to L.A."

Jayne didn't know what to think. Reilly's expression was inscrutable. There was definitely tension between them—it was almost palpable—but what it meant, she couldn't begin to guess. Was he really going to try to sway her opinion of the movie? Or was he angry with her for thinking he might do something so unethical?

Out of habit she ran the fingers of her right hand over her left wrist, but it was bare. The bracelet she had counted on to guide her so many times in the past was gone. She was flying blind, and she had the terrible feeling she was going to crash-land.

It was the longest two-hour drive in the history of motor travel. Reilly insisted on driving, which left Jayne with nothing to do but hang on to her hat, a green straw number with pink braid trim. She clamped it to her head with a gloved hand as Reilly sent the MG screaming down Highway 1.

"I didn't come courtin' you for reviews," he said above the whine of the engine. A muscle worked convulsively in his granite jaw.

"I didn't say you did," Jayne shouted. She checked her seat belt and tugged down the lace scarf that trimmed the neck of her English garden print dress, tucking it beneath her shoulder harness so it wouldn't catch in a wheel spoke and strangle her.

"You thought it," he said accusingly, narrowing his eyes at the way his pride stung.

Jayne stared out the windshield, hoping she didn't look as guilty as she felt. "You're a mind reader now? I didn't think you believed in ESP."

"I don't. It was written all over your face when you read that stupid article."

He down-shifted for a hairpin turn, holding back the rest of the conversation until they were back on a relatively straight stretch of road. He chanced a glance at her then and gave her a sardonic version of his famous grin. "Never mind that I did the film to help out a friend. Never mind that I put my best into it. I'd do more good beatin' my head against a brick wall than tryin' to get a good review from you."

"Don't you dare say I don't like your acting," Jayne said, taking her hand off her hat just long enough to shake a finger at him. "We've been all over that. I think you're wonderful. The movies you've chosen to appear in are a different matter altogether."

"We've been over that, too," Reilly reminded her. "I had my reasons for making those movies, and they're good reasons. That's more than you can say."

"About what?"

"About why you gave up your dream of writing and directing. You're damn good, Jaynie. If you would have stuck it out, you would have made it. But you took an easy out instead. Life's a lot safer when you're watching from the sidelines, ain't it? It's easier to pick apart other people's hard work and dreams than it is to build your own."

Jayne pressed herself back into the seat, feeling as if Reilly had reached over and cuffed her one. She gasped. "I resent that."

"Yeah?" He flashed her a burning look. "Do you deny it?"

Jayne glared at him, then turned away and began to chant. "Oooommm . . . oooommm . . . oooommm . . ."

"Bloody hell," Reilly muttered, dragging a hand back through his wind-tossed hair. "Am I gonna have to listen to this caterwaulin' all the way?"

"I am attempting to right myself on my spiritual axis and find the center of the universe," Jayne explained primly, lifting her nose in the air only to be hit in the face with a bug. She turned and scowled at Reilly. "I should know better than to try with you around. You're a disruptive force in my field of life energy."

"Yeah. I oughta get a medal for that," he said.

They rode the rest of the way in silence.

Jayne sat staring out at the scenery, not really seeing the rugged coastline or the golden hills as the winding highway took them into Marin County. Her feelings had certainly taken a trampling today, she thought, allowing herself the luxury of self-pity for a few moments.

Life with Reilly. He didn't believe in any of the things she believed in. He bullied her at every opportunity. He hated what she did for a living, and he thought she was a coward. What a guy.

But she loved him, Jayne thought with a depressed sigh. She loved him for his tenderness, for his boyish charm, for his loyalty to the people he cared about. He wouldn't have been arguing with her about the choices she'd made if he didn't care about her. In his own rough way, he was as earnest in his convictions as she was in hers.

That thought provoked memories of her own ideals, memories of how determined she had been to succeed when she'd left Notre Dame and headed west. She'd been so enthusiastic when she'd set out to chase that rainbow. What had happened to that enthusiasm? What had happened to that dream?

The rainbow had faded. Her priorities had changed. Or had she let them go?

They entered the hubbub of the airport in silence, encased in a grim bubble of stillness amid the noisy confusion of passengers departing and arriving. Jayne stood by and guarded Reilly's duffel bag as he bought his ticket. She walked beside him in silence to his gate, where passengers were already boarding the plane.

She hated airports. They were such public places to express private good-byes. Good-byes that always had the potential of being final. Her last good-bye to Mac had been at an airport. She'd kissed him at the gate and waved as he'd disappeared down the tunnel to board a plane that had never brought him back.

She'd known a vague sense of dread that day. It

hung over her today as well, a black shroud of depression that threatened to smother her.

Reilly was leaving. He was going back to Hollywood where he was adored by nearly everyone. And she was staying behind to write what would undoubtedly be a scathing review of the movie he had worked so hard on. She couldn't escape the feeling that he wouldn't be coming back except to collect his dog and his Jeep.

"I've got to board, luv," he said softly, slinging his bag over his shoulder.

His heart ached at the thought of leaving. It ached at the expression on Jayne's face and the tears pooling in her eyes. He hated leaving her, especially this way, when they'd been fighting. That stupid bracelet of hers had her convinced something terrible was going to happen, and no doubt she thought he wouldn't be coming back. His heart wanted to give her some positive proof that his love for her was true, but it also wanted her blind trust.

Two fat tears slipped over the barrier of Jayne's dark lashes as she looked up at him.

"I'm sorry we had to fight," she whispered, more tears choking her voice. She and Mac had never fought. They had existed on a plane of spiritual harmony. She and Reilly fought all the time.

This was probably just another sign that they didn't belong together, she thought, her heart sinking lower still.

Reilly brushed one crystal drop from her cheek with the pad of his thumb. "A fight ain't the end of the world, Jaynie. We're friends, remember?"

He bent down and kissed her softly, his lips caressing hers with all the tenderness and love he could convey. Her small fists clutched at the worn leather of his jacket in an unconscious effort to hold him there while the flight attendant made the last call for passengers to board.

"Good-bye," he murmured against her lips.

Jayne watched him walk away, but she didn't wave. She stood at the window, her right hand rubbing absently at her left wrist, feeling half of her heart being pulled away from her as Reilly's plane taxied down the runway.

She loved Pat Reilly as she'd never loved anyone, but he was no more right for her now than he had been when she'd been MacGregor's wife and Reilly had been MacGregor's best friend. As she'd known from the first, his intensity had set her on fire, but now she was alone and so cold, she shivered as she turned and headed for the exit.

ELEVEN

" 'THERE HASN'T BEEN a bomb like this since Hiroshima,' " Alaina Montgomery-Harrison read aloud. She lowered the newspaper just enough so she could stab Jayne with a look.

Jayne came to her own defense halfheartedly. "Well, there hasn't been. *Deadly Intent* is the worst waste of film I've seen since *Ishtar*."

"You have an unfortunate penchant for bald honesty, Jayne," Alaina declared. She took a sip of the milk the diner waitress set before her and grimaced. "Gawd, I hate milk. If I ever see a cow in person, I'm going to go right over the edge."

"Maybe Reilly won't read the review," Faith Callan said, eyeing the golden-brown pancakes the waitress set before her. "You said he wasn't expecting a good review from you, so why would he read it?"

"He'll read it," Jayne said fatalistically. "He may not be expecting a good review, but he'll be hoping just the same. I know how his mind works. I know how hard he worked on this film, how he did it to help out a friend, how he's been going through this rough time and needs my support. I can hear him say it—Where I come from a man helps out his mates and that's that. He'll think I've betrayed him when all I was doing was my job."

She looked down at the plate the waitress slammed in front of her. Runny eggs and soggy toast that looked as if they may have had a close encounter with the kitchen floor. She looked up at the waitress, who glared at her.

"Bonzi," the woman snarled.

"Well, I have to hand it to you, Jayne," Alaina said with a sigh as she folded the entertainment section of the paper in half and laid it on the table. "You've managed to turn all of womankind against you in one fell swoop by panning Reilly's movie."

"But I said nice things about Reilly!" she wailed.

"You said he does what he can with a script

that would have been better printed on toilet paper. Jayne, couldn't you have just given the guy a break and called it a so-so-movie?"

"But it wasn't a so-so movie. It was a skunk. I couldn't compromise my standards on this movie just because Reilly is in it. That would have been selling out." But what good would her high standards do her when she was old and lonely? She swallowed down her tears and spoke her thoughts aloud. "Should Reilly have expected me to give in because of our relationship? No. I can't take personal factors into account when I review a film. It wouldn't be fair to the people who count on my column to steer them to a good movie or away from a bad one."

Faith chewed thoughtfully on a bite of pancake then dabbed syrup off the corner of her mouth with her napkin. "Jayne, do you really think Reilly expected you to do him a favor? Do you really think this will have any effect on your relationship at all? Maybe you're blowing this review thing out of proportion."

Jayne stared down at the newspaper, her eyes drifting over the splashy article on the premiere of *Deadly Intent*. The accompanying photograph showed Reilly waving to the adoring thousands outside the theater with one hand while he wrapped the other around the slender waist of his co-star, the disgustingly beautiful LaReina Shelby. There they were, hundreds of women ready and willing to fling themselves at Reilly's feet, ready to worship the ground he walked on, and two columns over she had called his movie a flatulent flop.

Why did she have to be so brutally honest, she wondered. And why did Reilly have to be so stubbornly loyal to people who made bad movies? And why couldn't she have fallen in love with a placid person like Mac instead of a bull in a china shop like Reilly?

He was right. It had been easier loving Mac. Loving Mac had been soothing and calming. Loving Reilly was like strapping her heart to a roller coaster—all breathtaking highs and belly-scraping lows.

"I guess you'll find out tomorrow night, won't you?" Faith said.

"What?"

"At the play. Reilly's going to be here, isn't he? It is opening night for *A Taste of Starlight*."

"Umm . . ." Jayne hesitated, realizing every ear in the place was trained on her. Advance tickets for the play had sold out within hours. The town had been buzzing for weeks about Pat Reilly's appearance to benefit the theater company. But two days had passed with no word from Reilly. He was supposed to be at dress rehearsal later that night. Jayne tamped down her own secret fears that he wouldn't show up and forced a wan smile. "Of course he'll be here."

Immediately the sounds of breakfast being ordered, served, and eaten resumed. Jayne breathed a sigh of relief.

"I'm glad you were able to talk Bryan into being Reilly's understudy," Faith said, sipping at her coffee. "He needs to get involved in something."

"I had to promise him he would never have to perform," Jayne said, hoping she wouldn't have to renege on that promise. "He wasn't very happy about having to fill in for Reilly at practice these past couple of days." She checked her watch and sighed. "As a matter of fact, he's at the theater now helping Timothy hang the new curtains. I told him I'd pick him up at ten. I guess I'd better go get him."

She pushed back her chair and slung the strap of her enormous purse over her shoulder. "Y'all coming to opening night?"

"Of course," Faith said with a smile. "Shane and I have front row seats."

"Us too," Alaina said, her lush mouth lifting at

one corner. "I, for one, happen to enjoy Reilly's performances—even the lethargic, lackluster ones."

Jayne made a face at her friend and left the restaurant just in time to see Deputy Skreawupp stick a citation on the windshield of her car.

"Failing to prominently display proof of insurance?" she questioned, staring in disbelief at the ticket.

"It's on the books, sweet cheeks," the big cop intoned in his Joe Friday voice, shaking his stubby pencil at her, "and I know those books eight ways from Sunday. You'd better get with the program, or I'll crack you like a rotten egg, and I can do it." He started to stalk off down the street, but turned back. "And another thing. *Deadly Intent* was the best movie ever made."

"Everybody's a critic," Jayne muttered as she climbed into the sports car.

She pulled up in front of the theater just in time to see Bryan being assaulted by a woman who'd mistaken him for Reilly. The woman had him by the collar of his shirt and was hopping up on her toes to pelt him with kisses as he tried to pull away. Timothy Fieldman danced around the fracas with his hands in the air.

"Oh, gosh! Oh, gee, Mrs. Meinhampf, that's

not Mr. Reilly! I'm going to have to call the police if you don't stop this outrageous behavior!"

Jayne pulled up with one front wheel on the sidewalk and blasted the horn. The diversion was enough to break Mrs. Meinhampf's concentration and allow Bryan to escape. He lost part of his chambray shirt in the process, but didn't look back as he vaulted over the door and into the passenger's seat, shouting, "Go! Go!"

They peeled away from the curb and headed out of town without looking back.

"Jayne," Bryan said, straightening his glasses. He plucked a scrap of paper out of the pocket of his torn shirt and jotted himself a note. "I love you like a sister, but don't ever ask me to do this again."

"I'm sorry," she said, giving him a worried look. She dug a hand into her purse and tossed out an array of strange objects, including a book on astrology, a camera lens, and half a dozen tubes of lipstick, before coming up with a lace-edged hanky. Dividing her attention between the road and her friend, she reached over and attempted to wipe the lipstick off Bryan's cheek.

"I never meant for things to get so crazy. Shoot, all I ever wanted was self-fulfillment and spiritual bliss."

"Oh, is that all?" Bryan asked dryly. He took

the hankie from her and directed her hand back to the steering wheel. "That's a pretty tall order, honey."

"What do you mean?"

"I mean, we can't orchestrate our lives, Jayne. We can't know what the future has in store for us. We have to take our happiness where we can get it. I thought you would have figured that out when you lost Mac."

"Well, . . . yes. I cherish the time I had with Mac. I cherish the time I've had with Reilly," she said reflectively as she turned the car in at her drive. "I only hope that wasn't all the time I'll ever get to have with him."

"You love him."

"I've loved him for a long time. There's just so many things I'm not sure of," she said miserably as she parked the MG haphazardly in the yard. She looked over at Reilly's Jeep, where Rowdy had been sitting in the driver's seat for two days diligently awaiting Reilly's return.

"You'll have the answers, the answers you need, honey," Bryan said. "Don't you trust your bracelet anymore?"

"I don't have it," she admitted. "Reilly took it away from me. He said I was silly to believe in it and he took it away from me."

A slow grin spread across Bryan's handsome face. His wise blue eyes sparkled with secret humor. "Don't worry about it. You'll get it back."

"You think it's going to try to tell Reilly something?" Jayne snorted. "Reilly wouldn't believe it if the chain wrapped itself around his throat and tried to choke him."

Bryan chuckled. "He's that stubborn?"

"At least."

"But you love him anyway?"

She rolled her eyes. "Maybe you should just hit me in the head with a brick."

Bryan leaned over and kissed her cheek. "Hang in there, sweetheart."

Candi was sitting at the kitchen table when they walked in, practicing her breathing exercises by panting on her newly painted lime-green fingernails. She looked up at Jayne and frowned. "Oh, it's you. The one person on the face of the earth who thinks Pat Reilly's films should be shredded and used as packing material."

"Did I get any calls?" Jayne asked.

"You had a death threat. I told them to call back later." She nodded her spikey head in the direction of a package on the table. "There's the mail. The box came express."

Jayne eyed the box warily. It looked ordinary

enough. The label was typed. The return address was a gift shop in Encino. She pulled a paring knife out of a drawer and slit the tape. Inside was a letter taped to a black box.

"'Dear Calamity Jayne,'" she read. "'If you think my film stunk, just wait until you get a whiff of the stink bomb you set off by breaking the tape on this package. Regards, Reilly.'"

"I don't smell anything," Candi said, sniffing the air.

In the next instant the room was inundated with an aroma so rank, it threatened to peel the paint off the walls. They ran from the kitchen out into the yard, choking and gagging. The noxious fumes rolled out behind them in a bilious green cloud.

Candi's eyes were watering so hard her mascara was running a muddy river down her cheeks. "Jeez, Jayne, good move," she said with a sneer.

"It wasn't my fault."

"It was your rotten review."

"It was Reilly!" Jayne shouted, stamping her small foot in aggravation.

All she'd done was her job, and everyone was treating her as if she were a villain. This was all Reilly's fault. And if she ever saw him again . . . she was going to kiss him senseless.

TWELVE

THEY WERE GOING to be playing to a packed house, so long as there wasn't a riot first, Jayne thought morosely as she peered out from between the edges of the stage curtains. Act One wasn't to begin for ten minutes yet and already every seat in the place was taken. The faces in the audience were alive with excitement and anticipation. Murmurs of Reilly's name rose above the general din and rippled across the surface to assault Jayne's ears.

There were 1,140 people sitting out there, each and every one of them waiting to see Pat Reilly. Pat Reilly who had yet to return from L.A.

She hadn't heard a word from him, not counting the stink bomb that had driven her from her home. He hadn't shown up for dress rehearsal. There had been no call, no letter, nothing. Jayne felt as if she'd been cut adrift, her emotional connection to Reilly severed by feelings of betrayal on both sides.

If only they could start fresh, she thought. If only they could start together to follow new rainbows. She'd thought of little else for the past few days—pursuing her abandoned dream of writing and directing movies, of directing Reilly in a really good film, a film worthy of his talents. But as show time drew near, she couldn't help but think that new rainbow was going to be washed away by a tide of regret before she had the chance to chase after it. She'd held back too long, watching other people live their dreams while she hesitated, calling her cowardice peace and contentment.

She was guilty of exactly the same thing she had accused Reilly of. She had a talent she had turned her back on. It had simply been easier to abandon her dream than to follow it. Chasing a rainbow meant taking chances, risking rejection, disappointment. But there was a wonderful treasure at the end of it if one had the courage to go after it.

It was a lot like falling in love.

"Oh, gosh, I'm so nervous, Miss Jordan," Timothy whined, flipping through the pages of instructions on his clipboard. "Are you sure these curtains are all right? I'm sorry they're not the ones you ordered. We hung them just as you instructed, but—"

"They're fine, Timothy," Jayne said a bit sharply. Her own nerves were just a little too frayed to contend with a stage manager who had the disposition of a poodle.

She eyed the filmy curtains and shook her head. They had ordered heavy brocade drapes. They had received white diaphanous sheers. It was a bad omen. Once the house lights went down the audience would be able to see everything that went on while sets were being changed and actors were taking their places. The whole mood of the play would be disrupted, but there was nothing to do about it now. Sheer curtains were better than no curtains at all.

"Dim the house lights at eight sharp," she instructed, "and bring up the spot on Desiree's bed. The curtain goes up on my cue."

"But Mr. Reilly isn't here yet!" Timothy exclaimed, his Adam's apple bobbing in his throat as if it were a cork. He fussed with the white tape holding his glasses together. "I certainly hope he gets here in time."

"I don't think we can count on that," Jayne said, her heart aching as she spoke the words. She checked her watch and blinked back tears as she felt the last of her hope slide away. "Please tell Mr. Hennessy to be ready. He'll have to go on in Reilly's place."

"Oh, dear. He isn't going to like this at all," Timothy muttered as he scurried away.

Jayne looked around the set, finally settling herself on the ornate brass bed. She smoothed the white satin coverlet with her hands, then smoothed the skirt of her dress. The black background scattered with purple-and-blue flowers was a brilliant contrast to the spread, but she didn't really notice. Her first production was about to begin, but she couldn't concentrate on it. Her cast was assembled in the makeup room, awaiting a last minute pep talk from her, but all she could think of was Reilly and how their paths had intertwined only to part.

Maybe that was simply their karma, she thought with a sigh of resignation. Or maybe she was turning her back on yet another dream. Love had been easy with Mac; there had been no risks to take. Reilly was a whole other breed of cat. He was rough and rowdy and stubborn and impulsive . . . and she loved him. She loved every hard, rough-hewn inch of him.

Determination sparked inside her and flamed

to life. She wanted Pat Reilly in her life. This was one rainbow she wasn't going to allow to fade away, because the treasure at the end of it was well worth fighting for. She had always longed for a place to call her own, a place where she felt safe and content. That place was in Reilly's arms.

Reilly hit the brakes, and his rented car skidded into a parking space near the side entrance of the theater. He checked his watch and swore. Seven minutes to eight. Nothing had gone right in the three days he'd been away from Jayne. Now he was going to be late for the play as well.

Almost nothing had gone right, he amended with a grin as he thought of the meeting he'd had with Jason Shikenjanski. The reclusive producer lived in the middle of bloody nowhere with not even a telephone link to the outside world, but the man was a movie genius, and it had been worth the trip into the mountains to meet with him.

He jogged up the steps and into the building, excitement stirring in his belly as he was greeted by the sounds of the theater—the backstage hustle and the murmurs of the audience. It was going to be a great night. Hell, it was going to be a great life, he thought, shoving his hands into the pockets of his pleated navy trousers.

The fingers of his right hand came into contact with Jayne's bracelet, and Reilly's smile turned wry. The crazy thing had been driving him nuts. He must have had some kind of skin allergy to the gold or something. His fingers tingled every time he touched it. It had been practically burning a hole in his pocket ever since he'd taken it away from Jayne. And the longer he'd been away, the worse it had gotten. If he'd been as superstitious as Jayne was, he might have thought the thing was trying to remind him of her. As if he could ever get her out of his mind.

"Oh, Mr. Reilly! Oh, thank heaven you're here!" Timothy gushed, rushing toward him out of the wings. "I can't tell you how glad I am to see you! Mr. Hennessy was really angry when I told him Miss Jordan wanted him to get ready to go on. I can't even begin to tell you how unhappy he was. And all I could think of was, 'Don't kill the messenger—'"

"Jaynie did what?" Reilly's temper rose full-blown. His brows pulled down low over his eyes. A flush stained his high, hard cheekbones.

Timothy gulped hard. "She said it didn't look

as if you were going to get here in time, and so we should—"

"Bloody hell." He growled the words as he grabbed the stage manager by the scruff of the neck and gave him a shake. "Where is she?"

The boy's eyes bulged behind his glasses. "Oh, dear. Oh—she's—I believe she's on stage, Mr. Reilly, sir."

He let the boy go with a snarl and stormed toward the stage. When he saw Jayne, his anger shattered and fell away.

She sat on the bed with her dainty hands in the lap of her flowered dress, her head bent down, her wild dark hair spread out behind her. She looked all alone in the world. The sight of her wrapped around his heart and warmth surged through him. How many times had he looked at her and denied the feelings she stirred inside him? No more. He drank in the poignantly feminine picture she made in her dress with the puffed sleeves and snug bodice.

He loved her like he'd never loved another. She made him angry enough to spit tacks, but he couldn't imagine a future without her. She, however, had apparently been imagining a future without him.

"You haven't much faith in me, have you, sheila?" he said as he crossed the stage with his hands in his pockets.

"Reilly!" Jayne's head snapped up.

Her heart leaped into her throat and danced a frantic jig. She scrubbed the tears from her cheeks with the heels of her hands. Everything she'd felt dying inside her sprang instantly to life, revived by the mere sight of Reilly.

He was so handsome in stylish trousers and a polo shirt that matched the incredible blue of his eyes. A narrow leather belt with a silver buckle and tip emphasized his slender waist. His golden hair was neatly combed for once, and his expression was . . . disturbingly unreadable.

"I told you I'd be back, Jaynie. You didn't believe me?"

"When you didn't come back for rehearsal . . ." Jayne's words trailed off as she struggled with the explanation. "There was that picture in the paper and the review . . . and the stink bomb."

She cut herself off again and regrouped, summoning some righteous anger. "Well, what was I supposed to think? You left, and then the only word I heard from you drove me out of my house. I'm not liable to get that stink out of there for weeks!"

Reilly didn't try to fight his grin. "Yeah. That was a good one, eh? A bomb for a bomb."

Instead of laughing with him, Jayne sobered as she looked up at him. "What *was* I supposed to think, Reilly?"

He gave a shrug, his broad shoulders straining the knit fabric of his shirt. "That I was steamed about the review. You knew I would be. And I always send you a little something as a rebuttal; it's tradition. What did you think?"

Jayne didn't answer aloud. Every doubt she'd had over the past three days crossed her face. She was sure it was easy reading. Hitching his hands to his hips, Reilly sighed and his eyes saddened as he looked at her.

"You were supposed to know that I love you, Jaynie. You were supposed to believe in that love, not doubt me the minute I was out of your sight."

"But you'd accomplished what you'd come up here for—"

"Don't hand me that. I didn't come up here to exorcise ghosts or exact some kind of revenge or woo accolades out of a movie critic. I came up here to find out if the feelings I'd had burnin' inside me all this time were love. They are," he said decisively, his square chin jutting forward at an angle of challenge. "Do you doubt me now, Jaynie? Are you gonna call me on that?"

"I was afraid," she said, knowing it was a feeble excuse, but it was the truth. She'd been afraid of Reilly from the start, afraid of the feelings he'd awakened in her when she'd been married to Mac, afraid of his intensity, afraid of loving him, afraid of losing him.

"That's part of being in love, sweet." He delivered the news gently, as if to soften the blow. "I know it was different with you and Mac. I'm not Mac. I'm stubborn and ornery and I've a bloody bad temper."

"Tell me about it," Jayne said crossly. She shuddered at the memory. "You were so angry when you left here—"

"And I told you then, a fight ain't the end of the world. We've had our share of them in the past and I reckon we'll have our share in the future." He gave her a sexy, cocky grin and reached out to tweak her nose. "Hell, half the time I pick 'em just to see how cute you are when you're flustered."

Jayne gasped in outrage and crossed her arms beneath her meager bosom. "You're an absolute rascal. I don't know why I'd want anything to do with you."

"Because you love me," Reilly said simply. He

held up a hand to ward off her protest. "Don't bother denying it, luv."

Jayne narrowed her eyes and hissed at him. "You're an arrogant, bullheaded chauvinist."

"That's me," he said with a grin.

"That wasn't a compliment," Jayne declared, scowling at him. It was a scowl she had to work at to maintain. He was too blasted sexy, grinning at her in that thoroughly incorrigible way of his, that annoyingly cute dimple winking in his cheek. And it was difficult for her heart to ignore the fact that he had indeed returned. She reminded herself he was a day late and an explanation short. "Why didn't you call me?"

"Because I was in a meeting with Jason Shiken-janski, talkin' him into backin' a film." Reilly said with not the least hint of remorse for worrying her. She should have trusted him and she hadn't; worrying had been her penance as far as he could see. "The screenplay is excellent. The lead role is just the kind of thing I should have tried doing a long time ago," he said reflectively. "It'll take more time than I've ever had to give a part before, but I've been told by a very reliable source that I have the talent to do it—with the right director, of course, and I have the perfect one in mind. I think you might know her. I think you might be familiar with the script, as well. It's called *Everlasting* by Jayne Jordan."

Jayne was silent for a long moment as she looked up at the man she loved. All this time she'd thought they had nothing in common. But they shared a dream and a love. What more could she ask? Reilly was inviting her to face the future with him, to go down a new path together, a path they had both been afraid to face alone, a path that was suddenly bright with promise.

"I love you," she said simply.

Reilly nodded. The intensity of his gaze was focused full-power on Jayne as he asked, "And do you trust me, Jaynie? Come hell or high water?"

Reilly was a man of integrity. He was a man who made sacrifices for the people he loved. Jayne knew her own doubts had stemmed from old fears and insecurities. Now she dug down deep for the courage to put them aside and step on the roller coaster that life with Reilly would be. It would be a wild ride, but she would cherish every moment, secure in the knowledge that their love would bridge their differences.

"Yes," she said.

"Just like that?" he asked. "Don't you want to consult your astrologer or check with your bracelet first?"

Jayne shook her head and gave a little shrug, lifting her wrists to show they were unadorned. "Guess I just have to trust my instincts this time. You took my bracelet away, remember?"

"Oh, yeah. That reminds me." He pulled the gold chain from his pants pocket and reached out for Jayne's hand. "I believe this is yours," he said, circling her wrist with the bracelet and fastening the newly repaired clasp.

Jayne smiled as a warm, wonderful feeling flowed through her. It was wonder and love and contentment and excitement. It was a feeling that emanated from the golden links around her wrist and encompassed her whole being. She suspected Reilly was feeling it as well; there was a strange light in his eyes. But she knew wild horses couldn't have gotten him to admit it. She squeezed his fingers, loving every stubborn inch of him.

Her gaze fell to the gift Bryan had given her all those years ago, going over it link by intricate link, until she came to the dainty key. Beside it hung a new charm—a small golden heart set with a brilliant blue sapphire.

"That's to remind you," Reilly said, lifting her hand to his lips, tenderly kissing her knuckles, "that no matter where I go or what I do, you'll always have my heart, Jaynie. I'll always come back to you. You have my word on it."

And Jayne took what he said to heart, because she knew Pat Reilly was nothing if not a man of his word. He was making her a promise, a promise they could build a life on. It was time to put old ghosts to rest, to close the door on old fears, to turn together to chase a new rainbow.

"Marry me, Jaynie," Reilly said, his heart in his eyes.

"I will," Jayne answered, tears of love shining in her dark eyes.

Reilly stroked his hand back through her hair and tilted her head back as he leaned down and kissed her with all the love and tenderness his soul possessed.

And the audience, who had been watching the entire scene through the sheer white curtain, enthralled from the moment the house lights had gone down at precisely eight o'clock, rose and gave a standing ovation.